Note to Readers

While the Harringtons and the people they meet are fictional, the events they encounter are based on historical fact. By the end of 1937, many people in America were recovering from the Great Depression, but others still couldn't find work and had lost their homes.

Families enjoyed seeing movies like *Snow White* and *The Revenge of Tarzan,* and the opening of trails on Mt. Rainier gave people in Washington State a new place to enjoy. People living in Seattle during the summer of 1938 experienced one of the hottest summers on record. And the prize fight that Frank wants to go to so badly actually took place in Seattle that summer.

The famous "War of the Worlds" radio broadcast fooled many listeners. Police stations were overwhelmed by phone calls from concerned residents, particularly on the East Coast, where the invasion supposedly took place. That program became one of the most famous broadcasts in radio history.

The American Adventure

CHANGING TIMES

Susan Martins Miller

BARBOUR
PUBLISHING, INC.
Uhrichsville, Ohio

© MCMXCVIII by Barbour Publishing, Inc.

ISBN 1-57748-510-6

Published by Barbour Publishing, Inc., P.O. Box 719, Uhrichsville, Ohio 44683
http://www.barbourbooks.com

 Member of the
Evangelical Christian
Publishers Association

Printed in the United States of America.

Cover illustration by Peter Pagano.
Inside illustrations by Adam Wallenta.

CHAPTER 1

Christmas Plans

"Boom!"

With a swift kick, three-year-old Eddie Harrington knocked down the tower of wooden blocks he had spent twenty minutes building. Cubes of blue and red and yellow sprayed around the front room. He giggled with delight, obviously pleased with what he had done.

"Did you make another bomb?" His twin sister Barb hung her legs over the side of a dining room chair and looked on with approval.

"Yep," Eddie answered proudly.

"That was a good one."

"I'm the boss, and the people in my factory have to do what I say."

Twelve-year-old Isabel sighed and propped up one elbow on the dining room table across from Barb. She rested her chin in her hand.

"I don't think you understand what a bomb is," Isabel said.

"It blows things up. Boom!" was Eddie's response.

"Well, yes, you have that part right," Isabel responded. "But nobody blows up their own factory like you just did."

"I can if I want to!"

"Yes, you can. They're your blocks and it was your building."

Audrey, seven years old, raised her dark eyes from her cutting project. "Bombs are dumb. Everybody knows that. People should not be allowed to go around blowing up factories."

"I agree. A lot of people can get hurt in a bomb," Isabel said. She slid another sheet of white paper across the table to Audrey. "How's that snowflake coming along?"

Audrey carefully unfolded her paper and showed the intricate design she had cut into the paper. Everything that Audrey did was careful and thorough. She had cut slits into the paper in a complex pattern that was now perfect.

Mama came into the room just then. "Audrey, did you cut that all by yourself?" Her blond hair bounced as she smiled at her daughters.

Audrey nodded proudly. "Isabel is going to help me put our snowflakes up in the window."

"That will make the apartment look like Christmas," Mama said enthusiastically. "Make as many as you can."

"I'm going to make a hundred!" Audrey declared. She reached for another sheet of paper and began folding it in half, then in quarters, then in eighths.

Isabel laughed. "I don't think we have enough windows for a hundred snowflakes."

"Well, at least fifty," Audrey insisted.

Ed had once again built a quick tower of blocks and now swung his foot vigorously. "Boom!" He lost his balance and ended up on his bottom among the scattered blocks.

Barb giggled and slid out of her chair and went to help gather the blocks.

Mama scowled and shook her head. "We should be more careful what we talk about," she said. "Eddie has overheard things he doesn't understand."

"He knows that bombs blow things up," Isabel said, sighing.

"Yes, but he doesn't understand how angry the people are who set off those bombs. But even as angry as they are, blowing up factories is wrong!"

"They are union people, aren't they? Like Grandpa was?"

Mama sat down in a chair next to Isabel. "My father was a union officer thirty years ago. Back then, the unions were fighting for safe working conditions and decent wages so they could support their families. Now the unions are fighting with each other about how much money they're allowed to make. A lot of people are getting hurt in the process."

"There have been three bombs this month," Isabel said. "They should at least try to get along with each other at Christmastime."

"We should pray that 1937 will be the last year of these arguments," Mama said, "and that 1938 can get off to a prosperous, peaceful start."

"I hope so, too, Mama."

Mama stood up again. "I haven't got time to sit around worrying about the unions. Ever since we moved into this bigger apartment, I'm never caught up on the housework. There is always something that needs doing."

"I'll help you," Isabel offered. "Shall I do the dusting?"

"No, thank you," Mama said. "The best thing you can do for

me right now is keep the other children occupied." She looked around the room. "Where is Frank? He could be helping you."

"He said he had a headache," Isabel answered, "and went to lie down."

Mama sighed. "Not again. Poor Frank. He seems to catch every infection that comes around."

A knock came on the door. Isabel jumped up.

"That will be Yoshiko. She said she was coming over. She's working on a Christmas surprise for her mother, so she's coming here to do it."

"Oooh," Mama said, her blue eyes twinkling. "I'm curious now."

Isabel crossed the room and opened the apartment door. For three and a half years, her family had lived in the Fairfax apartment building that Yoshiko Wakamutsu's parents owned. For the first two years, the nine members of the Harrington family had crammed themselves into four rooms of a fourth-floor apartment. They were grateful to have any space at all after driving across the country from Minneapolis to Seattle with no guarantee that Daddy would get a job.

But Daddy did get a job. He worked at Boeing, helping to design airplanes. After two years in the small apartment, the Harringtons had moved into a double-sized apartment on the second floor. Now they lived just above Yoshiko's family. Yoshiko's mother, Idori Wakamutsu, occasionally invited all the Harringtons downstairs for a traditional Japanese meal of miso soup, tofu, rice, fish, and assorted steamed vegetables. And in return, Lydia Harrington, Isabel's mother, treated the two families to the bratwurst and sauerkraut that she had loved as a child growing up in a German family.

Isabel opened the door. "Hi, Yoshiko!"

Yoshiko glanced over her shoulder before she entered the Harrington apartment.

"Your mother didn't see you, did she?" Isabel asked.

"I don't think so," Yoshiko answered. She reached under her coat and pulled out a bundle wrapped in a cloth.

"What have you got there?" Mama wanted to know. She peeked over Isabel's shoulder at the mystery bundle.

"It's a bamboo box I made at Japanese school," Yoshiko explained. "I want to paint a design on it. But I want it to be a surprise for Mama-san at Christmas."

Mama gestured toward the dining room table. "Welcome to the art station. Audrey will be glad to share her supplies with you. Won't you, Audrey?"

Audrey looked up and considered the question for a moment before nodding her head.

"Mama, when are we going to get a tree?" Audrey asked. She opened up her latest paper snowflake to inspect it.

"My goodness, it's a whole six days until Christmas," Mama said. "Let's be patient a few more days."

"I really want a tree," Audrey insisted.

"And you will have one," Mama promised. "If we put up a tree too early, it takes all the excitement out of Christmas Eve."

"Christmas Eve! We have to wait until Christmas Eve?" Audrey protested.

"I'm going to stay up all night on Christmas Eve," Isabel said.

Mama raised her eyebrows as she picked up the dust rag she had left on the table. She wiped off a windowsill.

"I suppose you have it all planned out," Yoshiko said, knowing that her friend had a scheme for every occasion.

Isabel nodded as she straightened the stacks of paper Audrey had spread around the table.

"Boom!" came Ed's voice in the background.

"Still bombing?" Yoshiko asked.

Isabel nodded.

"Back to my plan. I'm sure there will be spectacular music on the radio. After all, it will be Christmas Eve. They are bound to plan a whole evening of carols."

"You sure like your radio," Yoshiko observed.

"You find out a lot of things by listening to the radio," Isabel answered. "But I'm sure on Christmas Eve they will have music. And I'll really like that. I'm going to listen for the whole evening, starting right after supper."

"And then?"

"Then it will be time to go to the eleven o'clock service at church. We always go. Even the little ones try to stay awake for that. We all get so excited that it takes hours to get everyone calmed down again. Eddie and Barb fall asleep on the way home, of course, but everyone else comes home and has a big snack."

"I remember that you did that last year!" Yoshiko said. "You wanted me to come up, but I was already sleeping."

Isabel nodded. "Maybe you could come this year, though. You could come to church with us. Couldn't she, Mama?" Isabel turned to her mother with an expectant face.

"We'll have to see what Mrs. Wakamutsu says about that."

"They could all come," Isabel continued. "Their church doesn't have a Christmas Eve service. They can come to ours."

"We'll keep that in mind," Mama said.

"And after your snack?" Yoshiko prodded.

"Well, then I'll probably have indigestion, and I won't be able to sleep. So I'll sit by the window and watch the snow."

Yoshiko laughed. "It hardly ever snows at Christmas in Seattle."

"It will this year. I'm sure of it."

Yoshiko laughed again. "Your dreams are like bubbles on the water."

"Another of your Japanese expressions? What does that one mean?"

"It means that it's pointless. You are hoping in vain. It's not going to snow on Christmas morning."

"The Japanese are not right about everything," Isabel answered. "It could snow."

"So you're going to sit up all night and watch for it?" Yoshiko looked doubtful.

"Certainly. And then I'll start making breakfast. Eddie and Barb will be up early, and probably Frank and Audrey, too."

"I'm going to be the first one up!" Audrey declared.

"Except for me, that is," Isabel said, "because I'll be up all night."

Audrey held up another snowflake. "Yoshiko, have you been to see *Snow White and the Seven Dwarfs*?"

A sly smile crossed Yoshiko's lips and her dark eyes narrowed. "As a matter of fact, I did see it. I took my brothers a few days ago."

Audrey put her scissors down. "Was it absolutely wonderful?"

Yoshiko nodded. "You can't even imagine a movie so grand," she said.

"Yes, I can. I have a good imagination."

"This was even better than anything you could imagine," Yoshiko said. "The music, the pictures, the handsome prince— it was all wonderful, and so romantic."

Audrey turned toward her mother, who was dusting around a vase in the corner of the front room. "Mama, when are we going to see *Snow White and the Seven Dwarfs*?"

Mama tilted her head in a warning. "I've told you a dozen times this week not to whine and nag."

Audrey lowered her curly head. "Sorry, Mama. But I do want to see the movie."

"I know you do."

The apartment door opened. Alice and Steven came in. They had strange expressions on their faces.

"What's going on with the two of you?" Mama asked. "I thought you would be home long ago."

"We've been occupied," seventeen-year-old Alice answered. She took off her hat and set it carefully on a table near the door. Reaching into the closet for a hanger, she said to Steven, "Here, give me your coat."

Steven, two years younger, handed her his jacket.

"Occupied?" Isabel asked. "What were you doing?"

"Shhh!" Yoshiko scolded.

"But I want to know," Isabel insisted.

"It is Christmastime," Yoshiko reminded her, "a time for secrets. Do not ask too many questions."

Alice laughed. "Listen to your friend, Isabel. She is making a lot of sense."

"But you don't have any packages," Isabel continued.

Steven rolled his eyes. "Give up, Isabel. Our lips are sealed." He glanced at his mother. "Where's Frank?"

"Lying down."

"His headache is back? I'm going to go check on him."

"Let me know how he is doing," Mama said. "He tends to suffer in silence."

Once again the front door opened, and Daddy strode through. "Ah, my beautiful family is all here," he said, "plus one beautiful neighbor." He winked at Yoshiko.

"I'm just about finished here," Yoshiko said. She picked up the bamboo box and admired the row of tiny flowers she had painted across the top. "It's going to be a good Christmas."

Chapter 2
Attacked!

"Snow!" Barb and Eddie were bundled up and playing on the sidewalk in front of the apartment building. With one hand, Barb clutched a ragged doll Audrey had given her. With the other, she pointed to the sky with her declaration of snow. A pink scarf trailed behind her and down the back of her purple coat.

Isabel scanned the gray Seattle sky. The clouds were so thick she could hardly find the fading sun. It would soon be time for supper. It had sprinkled lightly earlier in the afternoon, and the wind was growing stronger. But there was no sign of snow.

"It's not snowing," Isabel informed the twins.

"But I see snow," Barb insisted.

Isabel looked up again. "That's just Mrs. Cimelli shaking out her rugs. You're seeing fur balls from her white cat."

"I wish it was snow," Barb sulked. "I want snow for Christmas."

"So do I," Isabel answered. "You're too little to remember Minneapolis. We had real snow there." She gently tossed a bright orange ball for Eddie to catch.

"The pictures of Christmas have snow," Barb insisted. "I saw Mama's cards on the table."

"I know, but they aren't pictures of Seattle."

"What city are they pictures of?"

Isabel shrugged. "Most of them are not real cities. They're just pictures."

"But Santa will come on a sleigh. He has to have snow."

Isabel hesitated. Was Barbara old enough to understand Santa was not real?

"Santa has his ways," she finally said. "Don't worry about him."

"It's not even cold enough to snow," nine-year-old Frank said. He always had a practical perspective. Frank concerned himself with the facts. He now sat on the stoop in front of the building, leaning his head against the wrought-iron railing. "We used to have snow, and we used to have a yard in Minneapolis, too."

"We'll have a yard again," Isabel said. "Mama says we're going to move into a house in a few months. They've been saving money ever since we came to Seattle."

Frank turned to his companion, nine-year-old Kaneko Wakamutsu. "I'll miss you when we move."

"I hope you are not going to move very far," Kaneko said. "I want to be able to see you every day."

The iron railing jiggled against Frank's weight. He pulled

himself away from it cautiously.

"I have to remember to tell Papa-san about the railing," said Kaneko. "I'm sure he will fix it as soon as he knows that it is coming loose."

"If Frank wouldn't lean on it so much, maybe it wouldn't be so loose," Isabel said.

"It's been this way for months!" Frank said in his own defense. "It's probably because of the way you jump over it when you come flying out the front door. You're not patient enough to walk down three steps and go around."

"It is no problem," Kaneko insisted. In his usual way, he was trying to keep peace between the Harrington siblings. "Papa-san will fix it. Maybe he will let me help."

"How can we have Christmas without snow?" Eddie wanted to know. He tossed the ball back toward Isabel. The throw was not high enough, and it bounced to the ground before she could grab it. The ball rolled toward the cement steps.

"We have Christmas every year without snow," Isabel assured Eddie as she scooped up the ball, "and this year will be no different. December 25 comes no matter what the weather is."

"How many days until Christmas?" Barb asked.

"Four," Isabel answered. "We have to wait four more days."

"I can't wait," Barbara said. "Let's have Christmas tonight."

Isabel chuckled. "If it were up to me, I would have Christmas tonight."

"Don't be silly," Frank said. "You can't hurry up Christmas."

"Use your imagination, Frank," Isabel said, rolling her eyes.

"Don't you even care if you're right?" Frank retorted. "How would you like it if somebody decided to make your birthday four days earlier?"

"I know exactly when I was born. Nobody is really sure that

Jesus was born exactly on December 25," Isabel said. "His birthday could be on another day, and it would still be Christmas."

"It's still not right to change Christmas," Frank insisted stubbornly.

"Did you see those men who just went by?" Kaneko asked. He stood up and walked a few steps down the block. "I saw them yesterday, too."

"What men?" Isabel perked up. She was tired of arguing about Christmas and was glad for the change in topic. She threw the ball back to Eddie without paying any attention where it landed.

Kaneko pointed down the block. "There. I don't think they live around here. I've lived here my whole life, and I know everyone who lives in any of the buildings around here."

"Are you sure you know everyone?" Frank asked. "Maybe they're new."

Kaneko shook his head. "No. They don't live here. I wonder what they are doing."

Isabel peered down the block at the backs of the two men. Their coats were thin and tattered, and they had not shaved in days. They each carried a canvas bag slung over their shoulders. "They don't look like they live anywhere," she said.

"What do you mean?" Frank wanted to know. "Everybody lives somewhere."

Isabel shook her head. "Not those two men. I heard Alice talking about men like that with Mama the other night."

Frank respected everything seventeen-year-old Alice said, so he wanted to know more. "What do you mean, 'men like that'?"

"They call them 'indigents,' " Isabel explained. "They don't have a place to live, so they sleep in the streets or in empty buildings or wherever they can find a place to stay warm at night."

The two strangers were about two blocks away now. The children followed them with their eyes as far as they could.

"Hey! There's Daddy!" Isabel cried out. She lost interest in the strangers. "Look at all those packages he has. He's been Christmas shopping!"

Frank jumped up for a better view. "That's Daddy, all right. I can see the red scarf that he always wears."

Isabel laughed. "Mama knitted him a new blue one for Christmas, but I think he'll keep wearing the red one. He likes the way it looks with his tweed coat." She left the ball idle on the sidewalk. "Watch the twins, Frank."

And she was off. Daddy never shopped for any Christmas presents until right before Christmas. Some years, he did not shop at all. For the last few years, there had not been many packages under the Harrington tree, and the ones they opened contained practical items that Mama had made herself. Sometimes there would be a hand-me-down from an older relative. The depression that started when Isabel was Ed and Barbara's age had forced her parents to keep the family on a tight budget. Mama managed to find enough wool yarn for a new pair of socks or a new scarf at Christmas for each of her children. And on Christmas Day, everyone in the family got to eat an entire orange without sharing it with anyone else.

But this year was different. Daddy had been working at Boeing for more than three years. Alice worked full time now and gave Mama most of what she earned. The family had recently moved to a larger apartment. Isabel had already discovered a pile of small packages behind the canned goods in the pantry. She had supposed that was all there would be, and it was all she could do to keep herself from peeling back the edge of the paper to see what might be in the boxes. Now here came Daddy with his arms full of brightly colored boxes of all sizes.

Isabel took off down the block at a steady trot. Mama sometimes told her that at twelve years of age she was getting too old to be running through the streets of Seattle like a maniac. But Mama's eyes always twinkled when she said that. Isabel had long ago decided that Mama was simply jealous because she really was too old to do what Isabel did.

About a block away from her father, Isabel slowed her steps slightly. She was just about to call out and wave when she realized her father was not watching her. Daddy had stopped walking and was talking with the two strangers who had passed the apartment building a few minutes earlier. The holiday smile that he had been wearing for weeks faded from his face as he looked intently into their unshaven faces. He shifted his load of packages. He looked nervous.

Isabel examined the strangers again. Even from a block away she could see the tattered state of their clothes. They both needed haircuts rather badly. One man's shoe flapped open at the sole every time he moved his foot. The other had no buttons on his coat.

The taller man took a small package off the top of the pile, shook it against his ear, then dropped it into a canvas bag he carried. A leer on his face dared Daddy to try to stop him. Daddy did not protest. His face lost its rosy color.

Indignation rose up within Isabel. How dare that man take one of the family's gifts? Why would Daddy let him do that? Suddenly she realized what was about to happen. She spun around on one foot and screamed, "Frank! Get help!"

Frank was already on his way up the steps. He, too, had seen what was happening. "Where's your father?" he frantically asked Kaneko.

He did not wait for an answer. Yanking open the front door, he charged through the lobby looking for Mr. Wakamutsu. The landlord was nowhere to be seen.

Ignoring the rules, Frank ran around behind the big reception desk and banged on the office door. No one answered. He jiggled the door knob. It was locked. Mr. Wakamutsu must have finished his paperwork for the day.

Frank wheeled around and charged down the hallway to the Wakamutsu apartment. He thumped on the door politely at first. But when no one came to the door immediately, he curled his hand into a fist to pound. After he struck the door three more times, Kaneko's little brother, Abiko, finally opened it.

"You are very rude!" Abiko exclaimed.

"Where's your father?" Frank gasped. "Tell him to come! Quickly! Outside!"

Frank turned on his heel and charged toward the front door again. He heard the hurried footsteps of his landlord right behind him. Outside, a glance over the railing told him that Kaneko was looking after Ed and Barb, so Frank followed Mr. Wakamutsu up the street. He pumped his legs hard to keep pace.

His heart sank at what he saw. Daddy was lying on the sidewalk with his beige tweed coat in a slushy puddle. He had one hand pressed to the side of his forehead. Blood trickled between his fingers, and his eyes were closed. Isabel was bending over him, saying something that Frank could not hear. The packages were nowhere to be seen. The red scarf his father loved so well was gone as well.

Mr. Wakamutsu reached Daddy first, but Frank was not far behind.

"Donald, you are all right?" their landlord asked.

Daddy opened his eyes and reached out a hand toward his friend. "Takao, thank you for coming. Frank, you, too."

"I will help you," Mr. Wakamutsu said. He braced himself behind his friend's shoulders and helped the wounded man sit up.

"Did they hurt you, Daddy?" Frank asked. He crouched down to look at the wound on his father's head. Daddy's dark hair was matted down with blood. One eye was black, and his lip was split open in one corner.

Isabel turned to Frank. "Now do you see why Mama hates boxing so much?"

"It's not the same," Frank countered. Still, he was troubled by what had happened to his father at the hands of another man.

"I seem to have quite a headache," Daddy said, wincing at the pain of moving.

"I saw them punching you in the stomach," Isabel said to Daddy.

Daddy nodded ever so slightly. "I have my winter coat on, so they did not hurt me. But they did that to make me let go of the packages."

"They took everything!" Isabel cried. "They beat up Daddy and took our Christmas away."

"No one can take our Christmas away," Daddy said softly.

"The important thing is that Daddy is not hurt badly," Frank said.

"Can you stand up?" Mr. Wakamutsu asked.

Daddy swallowed hard and nodded. Leaning on Mr. Wakamutsu and Isabel, he pulled himself to his feet. He smiled thinly as he looked down the two blocks he still had to walk. "Home, sweet home, here I come."

CHAPTER 3
Frank's Idea

"Lean on me, Daddy," Isabel said as she put an arm around her father's waist.

They took small steps. Daddy winced with each one. Isabel nearly stumbled under his weight.

"I must have twisted my ankle when I fell," Daddy said.

Isabel felt his weight on her shoulder. He was favoring his left foot. She glanced up at his face and saw that blood was still trickling from the cut on his head

"I have good Japanese remedy," Mr. Wakamutsu said.

Frank walked alongside the threesome. "I'm sorry you got

hurt, Daddy," he said. "We saw that you had packages. We were coming to help you."

"Too bad we didn't get there a little sooner," Isabel said.

Daddy managed a thin smile. "I'll admit that I had a good time shopping for all of you this year. I'm sorry I won't get to see the looks on your faces when you open up those boxes. I'm afraid I can't afford to replace them."

"It's okay, Daddy," Isabel said. "We'll get to see the look on your face when you open our presents." With the red scarf gone, Daddy was going to need the new blue scarf Mama had knitted him.

They were only a block away from their building now. The twins were standing in front, pointing down the sidewalk at their father.

"The twins!" Isabel exclaimed. "I forgot all about them."

"It's all right," Frank said. "Kaneko is watching them."

Isabel could see that the rambunctious three-year-olds were trying their best to burst out of Kaneko's control and run down the street. They kept turning their heads toward Kaneko and pointing at their father. Isabel and Mr. Wakamutsu had worked out a system that let Daddy almost hop his way home without putting much weight on his sore ankle.

"I'd better go tell the others what happened," Frank said.

"That's a good idea," Isabel agreed. "You'd better get Mama."

Frank trotted ahead of the threesome. The twins almost attacked him as soon as he got within reach.

"What happened to Daddy?" Barb demanded.

"Daddy's hurt!" Eddie exclaimed.

"Yes," Frank said, as he took the twins by their hands, "Daddy is hurt but not very badly."

"What happened?" his friend Kaneko asked, falling into step beside Frank.

Frank looked down at the small faces of Eddie and Barb.

"Do you two know what a bully is?" Frank asked as he walked toward the steps.

Barb nodded. "It's a very mean person who makes you do things you don't want to do."

Frank nodded. "That's what happened to Daddy. He ran into some bullies on the way home. They knocked him down."

"But why?"

"He had some packages, and they wanted them."

"But those packages are for us," Eddie protested.

"They were, but now someone else will have them," Frank answered.

"That's not fair!"

"No, it's not," Frank agreed. "But it happened, so we have to make the best of it. We need to go find Mama."

Kaneko yanked open the front door, and they all went inside. They headed down the hall to the back stairs, went up one flight, and opened the apartment door.

Mama was sitting at the dining room table. She had just finished tying a bow on a package. "There you are!" she said brightly. "I was beginning to wonder if you were ever going to come back inside. Where's Isabel?"

"She's still outside," Frank explained. "There's been—"

But Barbara could not wait to tell the news. "Some bullies beat up Daddy!"

Mama stood up immediately. "What? Is that true, Frank?"

Frank nodded glumly. "But he's all right, Mama. Isabel and Mr. Wakamutsu are helping him home."

"Steven!" Mama called.

He appeared immediately. "I heard. I'll go right out."

"I'm coming, too," Mama said. She turned to Frank and Kaneko. "You two stay right here, do you hear me?"

"Yes, ma'am."

23

Mama and Steven flew out the door without even reaching for their coats.

Frank looked down at Eddie and Barb, who both looked a little stunned.

"Daddy is okay," he promised them. "I saw him for myself."

Mama and Steven were back almost right away. Isabel, Daddy, and Mr. Wakamutsu had reached the building. Mama and Steven took over for Isabel and Mr. Wakamutsu and helped Daddy climb the wooden steps one at a time. Frank could see that Daddy really did not want to step on his left foot at all now. Leaning on Mama and Steven, he hopped up each step, wincing and breathing heavily.

Isabel helped open the door wide, and at last they all made it into the front room. Daddy lowered himself into a comfortable chair with a heavy sigh.

Steven pushed a footrest in front of the chair and helped Daddy lift his foot and stretch it out in front of him.

"Are we going to call the police?" Isabel asked. "We saw the men. Kaneko has seen them before. We could help find them and bring them to justice."

"I'm not quite feeling up to pursuing justice," Daddy said. "Maybe in a little while."

"But the trail will be cold!"

Steven darted a look at Isabel that told her to change the subject or stop talking at all.

"Isabel, bring some ice please," Mama said. "Frank, help her chip it off."

The two of them went to the kitchen and opened the icebox. They stared at the block of ice in the bottom, below the food shelves. A solid block of ice that melted slowly was the best way to keep the food fresh, but it made their task difficult.

"This could take a while," Frank said.

"Just get the chisel, and let's get started," Isabel said.

Frank held the chisel steady in a corner of the ice block while Isabel tapped on the end of it with a small hammer. At last the corner began to crack and crumble. Isabel snatched up a dish towel and began collecting the odd-sized chips in it.

"Do you think that's enough?" Frank asked.

"A little more," Isabel said. "His foot is really beginning to swell."

A few minutes later, they were satisfied and tied the ends of the dish towel around the ice chips.

In the front room, Daddy was sprawled in the chair with his foot up and his head back. Mama took the ice pack from Isabel and handed it to Steven.

"Daddy, does your head hurt?" Frank asked.

Daddy nodded slightly.

Mama wiped Daddy's head with a damp cloth while Steven held the ice pack against Daddy's ankle.

Frank turned to his neighbor. "Mr. Wakamutsu, you said you had a good Japanese remedy."

Mr. Wakamutsu nodded. "If the ice does not help, I will fix special tea."

"Donald, would you rather lie in your bed?" Mama asked.

Daddy shook his head. "I don't want to move right now."

"Here's a pillow for behind your back," Isabel said, as she tucked the pillow into the corner of the chair.

"You're all too kind," Daddy said. "I'm sure I'll be fine if I just sit still for a little while."

"Daddy, can I sit in your lap?" Barb asked.

"Not now," Isabel answered, "we need to let Daddy rest."

Daddy waved his hand. "Let her come. Let them both come."

Grateful for the invitation, Barb and Eddie climbed up into Daddy's lap and snuggled against his chest. He folded his arms around their shoulders. For a moment, Isabel was jealous, wishing that she were still small enough to do that.

Daddy sighed. "I'm sorry about the lost packages. I was planning a very nice Christmas for you all this year. But one thing bothers me even more than that."

"What's that, Donald?" Mama asked.

"It's very sad that there are people here in our own city— even in our own neighborhood—who are so desperate that they would steal Christmas presents. They don't even know what's in those boxes, but they took them anyway."

"The depression has been hard," Mama said. "We're fortunate. Except for a few months in 1935, you've always had a job. Now we're able to start saving a bit of money again. We may even be able to buy our own house. But not everyone is so lucky."

"That's my point," Daddy said. "I wish there was something that we could do for people like those two young men."

Mr. Wakamutsu shook his head mournfully while Mama and Steven sighed. Isabel glanced at Frank. His lips were moving in and out, a sign that he was thinking hard about something.

"Isn't there?" Frank asked.

"Isn't there what?" Daddy said. Barb squirmed in his lap to hug him more closely.

"Isn't there anything we can do?" Frank responded.

"Well, I suppose I have to admit that I haven't given it any serious thought."

"But if you want to do something, then you have to think of something to do," Frank insisted.

Daddy moved the cold cloth off his eyes and looked at his middle son. "You're absolutely right, Frank. But I have a headache right now. How about if you do the thinking?"

"All right, I will."

"Isabel, get your father a fresh cloth for his face," Mama instructed. "Barb, Eddie, it's time to get down now."

Frank looked at his father, with his head on the back of the chair and the cloth over his eyes. Mama had put a white bandage on the cut on his forehead, and as long as Daddy did not move his foot, it seemed not to bother him too much. If Daddy meant what he had said about trying to help the people who had hurt him, they would have to come up with some good ideas. Frank worked his lips while he thought. Isabel came back with a fresh cool cloth for her father's face.

"How about if we give Christmas presents to those people who don't have homes?" Frank said.

Everyone turned to look at him.

"Daddy said he wanted to help them. He asked me to think of some ideas. That's my idea."

Daddy sat up a bit straighter. "And it's a good idea. When those men open the boxes they took from me, they are going to find some things that they have no need for. Why not give them some things they do need?"

"Like warm socks," Frank said, "or scarves." He looked at his mother and winked.

"Right," Daddy said, "or some tins of food."

"Will you help us, Mr. Wakamutsu?" Frank asked.

Mr. Wakamutsu nodded enthusiastically. "Everybody will help. The whole building."

"That's right," Frank said, "we can get everyone in the whole building—or the whole block—to contribute something to the packages."

"We can tie them up with ribbon and take them out on Christmas," Isabel said.

Frank was nodding in agreement. "But you know what, Daddy? The real problem is not Christmas. Those men would not have stolen our Christmas packages if they had the things they need the rest of the time."

Daddy raised his eyebrows. "You're absolutely right, Frank. We have to do something about the rest of the year. Then maybe next Christmas, what happened to me today will not happen to someone else."

"Aren't you getting carried away?" fifteen-year-old Steven asked. "You're going to need a lot of money to do what you're talking about."

"We'll ask people to be generous," Daddy said.

"But you can't help all the indigent men in Seattle," Steven argued. "There are too many of them."

"Maybe not," Daddy said, "but we can help the ones we see around our own neighborhood."

"Those men don't live around here," Isabel reminded her father. "They are not our neighbors."

"Who is our neighbor?" Daddy challenged her.

"People in our neighborhood," Isabel answered logically.

"What if the Good Samaritan had said that?" Daddy asked Isabel.

"Do you mean the story in the Bible?"

"Right. The Samaritan saw a man who had been beaten up a lot worse than I was. And he helped, even though the man was a stranger. Why shouldn't we do the same thing?"

"You want to help even the men who beat you up?

"Even them. They were walking through our neighborhood," Daddy responded. "That makes them our neighbors." He turned back to Frank. "Son, you have a great idea. As soon as I get rid of this headache, you and I are going to sit down and figure out how to do this."

"I will go make tea," Mr. Wakamutsu said. "It will make your headache go away."

CHAPTER 4

A Japanese Feast

"Osechi-ryori?" Frank squished up his face with his question. He was not sure he had said the word correctly. "What is that?"

"It's the special New Year's foods that Japanese people eat," Kaneko responded proudly.

Frank opened the apartment door wider so his friend could come in. As Kaneko entered, Frank leaned over slightly to sniff the dish he carried. "It's sweet black beans," Kaneko explained. "One of my favorites."

"I'm not so sure about that," Frank said cautiously.

"You must eat one bean for every year of your age," Kaneko

said. "That is the tradition. But I always go back for as much as Mama-san will let me have."

Frank glanced down the hallway. "Where's the rest of your family?"

"They're coming."

The remaining four Wakamutsus appeared around the corner just then. Frank held the door open, and they all bowed slightly as they entered the Harrington apartment. Each of them carried a steaming dish of food.

"Hurry up," Abiko said. "This is hot."

"Everything is red and white," Frank observed as he examined each dish that went past him. "Did you do that to match the tablecloth Mama put out?"

"Those are the traditional New Year's colors," Yoshiko explained. She paused at the door long enough for Frank to get a good look at a dish of rice and fish.

"How did you make the rice pink?" he asked.

"By cooking rice with red adzuki beans," Yoshiko explained. "The tradition is that this brings happiness to your friends. And we want happiness for your family."

Isabel burst into the front room. "Good, you're here! I haven't eaten a thing all day so I would be hungry now." She hurried over to take the dish out of Yoshiko's hands.

"Then you must eat some long noodles," Yoshiko said, smiling, "so you may live to a ripe old age."

"Long noodles will do that?" Frank asked.

Yoshiko laughed. "I suppose not. But it is the Japanese tradition, so it is fun to pretend."

Isabel set Yoshiko's dish on the dining room table and returned to take one of the two dishes that Mrs. Wakamutsu carried. "Rice cakes! I love it when you make rice cakes!"

"Yoshiko tells me that is so," Mrs. Wakamutsu said. "So I made them."

"They are still hot, and we even have the soybean powder," Yoshiko said.

"Thank you!" Isabel cried as she carried the dish to the dining room table.

Mama had put out a red tablecloth and white napkins. In the center of the table was a bowl of red cinnamon candies, surrounded by tall white candles.

"Greetings, Wakamutsus," Mama said as she came from the kitchen. "Is everybody ready for a New Year's feast?"

Three-year-old Eddie rested his chin on the table. He inspected the dishes spread out before him. "I'm hungry. But I don't like Japanese food."

"You've never even tried it," Isabel said. "Try to have a sense of adventure."

"Yuck!"

Mama looked around. "Everything is ready. Where are Steven and Audrey and the others?"

In a few minutes, both families gathered around the Harrington dining room table where the food was arranged buffet-style. Isabel could hardly keep her eyes closed while Daddy asked God to bless the food and gave thanks for the New Year and the Harringtons' friendship with the Wakamutsus. Finally he said, "Amen."

"Dig in!" seven-year-old Audrey exclaimed.

Eddie was the only one who hesitated. He stood with a plate in his hand, pouting slightly, while the others pressed past him to get to the food. Steven urged the Wakamutsus to fill their plates first. Isabel watched carefully how they arranged their food on the plates.

"I don't have to use chopsticks, do I?" Frank asked, as he served himself nine of the sweet black beans, one for each year of his life.

Yoshiko laughed. "We'll let you use a fork."

31

"I can't figure out the chopsticks," Frank moaned. "I'm not even going to try." He put some of the red rice on his plate.

Isabel picked up a pair of sticks and nimbly moved them around with her fingers. "It's easy. You just have to practice."

"I'll stay with my fork," Frank said. His plate full, he went to take a seat in the front room and balanced his plate on his knees. Kaneko sat next to him with his plate loaded down with beans.

"You're a lot older than you look," Frank observed.

Kaneko laughed and shoved a forkful of beans into his mouth.

"Has anybody made any New Year's resolutions?" Daddy asked as he came away from the table with his own plate full.

"I'm going to get straight A's in school," Steven announced.

Isabel groaned. "That's nothing new. You've done that before."

"Well, what are you going to do?" Steven challenged in return.

Isabel picked up a piece of fish with her chopsticks. "I don't know. I have to think about that some more."

"You could stop picking on poor Frank," Steven suggested.

Isabel ignored him and busied herself eating a rice cake.

"I'm going to learn how to make these rice cakes," Mama said, "that is, if Idori will teach me."

Mrs. Wakamutsu smiled. "I would be most happy to teach you."

"I'm going to take out more packages to the men," Frank announced.

Daddy nodded. "That was one of the best Christmas Eves we've ever had. And it's all thanks to Frank. He's the one who thought of doing something practical for some of the homeless men in Seattle."

Frank glowed. "You did most of the work, Daddy," he said.

Daddy shook his head. "Not true. You went around to all the neighbors in the building and collected the items. And you and Kaneko packaged them up with paper and string. All Mr. Wakamutsu and I did was to help deliver them."

"I never even got to see what you put in them," Isabel said.

Frank shrugged. "Toothpaste, tinned meats, combs, shoe strings, a few oranges. Things like that."

Mama nodded. "Those things are practical and healthy."

Frank smiled. "Mrs. Watson on the fourth floor also made eight dozen chocolate cookies."

Mama chuckled. "It was Christmas, after all!"

"Isabel fell asleep on Christmas Eve," Audrey reminded everybody. "She was going to stay up all night, but she fell asleep on the sofa."

Isabel darted a look at her younger sister. "Mama said I had to be quiet, and it's hard to stay awake if you can't make noise."

Daddy looked at Frank. "So you want to take more packages?"

"We could put something else in them," Frank said. "But I don't want to stop."

"What other ideas do you have?" Daddy wiped his mouth on his napkin before taking another bite of rice and fish—with a fork.

Frank swallowed a bit of rice cake. "I've been thinking about that. What good is a Christmas package if those men have nothing else the rest of the year? We can help them all the time."

"But how?" Daddy wanted to know.

"I'm sure Mrs. Watson would make some more cookies. Mrs. Sawada said she would help again, too. I was thinking that each family could adopt one of the homeless people for the year."

"Hey! That's a great idea!" Daddy responded enthusiastically.

Frank turned to Mr. Wakamutsu. "You know where some

of them sleep at night. I heard you say that."

Mr. Wakamutsu nodded. "There is hotel a few blocks away. It is a flophouse for many men."

"We could go there," Frank said, "with packages every few weeks. We could find out what things they really need and try to collect those things."

Isabel wrinkled her nose. "They need some clean clothes. That's what they need. They stink!"

"We could do that," Daddy said. "I could talk to some of the men I work with and see if they have old clothes they don't wear anymore."

"I could mend things that are torn," Mama volunteered. "Just because they don't have homes, they don't have to wear rags."

Steven set his plate on an end table and leaned back in his chair. "Do you really think you can do this?" he asked.

All the eyes in the room turned to him.

"There are a lot of homeless men in Seattle," Steven said. "It's in the news all the time. It's a big problem. There aren't enough jobs for all of them. So can you really do anything about a problem that the city government doesn't know how to fix?"

"I can start with the men Mr. Wakamutsu knows," Frank said confidently. "Maybe those are the only ones we'll be able to help, but at least we'll be doing something."

"I don't want you going to that flophouse alone, Frank," Mama said as she scraped the last of her rice across the plate with her chopsticks.

"Your mother is right, Frank," Daddy said. "We'll each have our responsibilities. You can talk to the neighbors. Mr. Wakamutsu and I will make deliveries."

"But I want to help!" Frank protested.

"Not the first time, Son," Daddy said. "Let me go first and see if it's safe for you."

"But how do you know if it's safe for you?" Frank said.

"I'll be fine," Daddy assured Frank, as he also lifted his eyes to Mama. "We'll work this through together."

Nearly everyone had finished eating. Even Eddie, sitting on the floor with his plate in front of him, seemed satisfied with the unfamiliar Japanese food.

"Isabel," Mama said, "perhaps you can begin taking some of these plates to the kitchen."

"Yoshiko will help," Mrs. Wakamutsu said, looking firmly at her daughter.

The girls glanced at each other with a sigh and began their task. They had to make several trips back and forth to the kitchen to clear the plates from fourteen people.

"The next thing Mama will say is that I should rinse the dishes," Isabel said, and she reached for the faucet. "So I might as well do it now."

Yoshiko nodded. "I'll help you."

"You didn't say what your New Year's resolution is," Isabel said as she rinsed the first plate under the running water and set it in the bottom of the sink.

Yoshiko handed Isabel another dish and tilted her head thoughtfully. "I think I might volunteer at the Japanese school."

"Really?" Isabel said. "When you started going for Japanese lessons, you hated it."

"I don't anymore. Our family does not believe in many of the Japanese traditions because we are Christians. But it is still interesting to learn about them."

"Like good health coming from eating beans?"

"Right. But I don't want to throw away the spoon."

Isabel jumped and peered into the kitchen trash can. "Did I throw away a spoon?"

Yoshiko laughed. "No. It's an expression."

"What does this one mean?"

"I don't want to give up," Yoshiko explained. "There are many good things to learn about Japanese culture. Now what about your New Year's resolution? Did you think of it yet?"

"Not yet." Isabel put some soap in the sink and began to fill the basin.

"Steven is right," Yoshiko said. "You could resolve not to pick on Frank so much."

"But it's so much fun to pick on Frank," Isabel protested. "He believes everything I tell him."

Yoshiko shook her head. "Soon he will stop believing anything you say. And then where will you be?"

"That's not going to happen."

Yoshiko picked up a dish towel and began drying plates. "It might. He's not a little boy anymore."

"Well," Isabel said cautiously. "I'll think about reforming. But can I play just one more trick?"

The corners of Yoshiko's mouth turned up. "I have a feeling you have a plan."

"I do have some ideas," Isabel said, "but we'll have to work out the details. Are you with me?"

"You're not going to hurt Frank, are you?"

"I never hurt Frank. He gets mad, but later he laughs at how funny things were."

"Okay. Count me in."

"This is what I was thinking. . ."

Barb pushed open the door. It hit the wall with a thud. "Mama says you should give me some milk," she announced.

Isabel winked at Yoshiko and turned to her little sister. "Sure, Barb, I'll get you some milk. Where's your favorite pink cup?"

Barbara produced it from behind her back. Isabel went to the icebox for the milk. Over her little sister's head, her eyes twinkled at her friend.

CHAPTER 5

The Prank

Frank pulled open the cupboard door once again to make sure he was looking in the right place. He had already looked three times. The combs were there, and seven tins of tuna, six cans of beans, and a bottle of aspirin. There were supposed to be seventeen tins of tuna. He was sure he had counted them carefully the night before. And six tubes of toothpaste had disappeared, too.

"Are you sure you put everything in here?" Kaneko asked, looking at the half-empty cupboard. They huddled together on the gray tile floor, staring at the inside of the dark cupboard.

"Positive," Frank insisted. "This is the cupboard your father said we could use to collect things. He was sitting right here at his desk when I asked him."

The boys were crouched behind the oversized wooden reception desk that greeted guests at the Fairfax. This was Kaneko's father's private territory. He rarely allowed anyone back there. Mahogany cupboards filled the wall behind the desk from floor to ceiling. Mr. Wakamutsu kept his hotel records locked away in some of them, and others were full of books. He had cleared out a large lower cabinet for Frank to store items that would be given to the homeless men. He said that Frank's project was so important that everyone should sacrifice, and he had given the boys permission to use the cupboard.

Kaneko turned his head from side to side. "All the cabinets look the same. Are you sure you have the right one?"

"I'm positive," Frank insisted. "Some of the things are here. Why would I put the rest somewhere else?"

Kaneko shrugged. "Maybe we should look in the other cabinets, just in case."

Reluctantly Frank agreed. They got up off their knees and began opening one door after another. They found papers, books, cleaning supplies, and broken toys, but no tinned tuna and no toothpaste. Kaneko circled around the area again and slammed all the doors closed.

"The stuff is not here," Frank said. "I don't understand what could have happened to it."

"Did you leave anything in your room?"

"No, I brought everything down right away so Eddie would not get into it."

"Well, maybe it will turn up before it's time to deliver the things to that other hotel," Kaneko said hopefully.

Frank sighed. "In the meantime, I want to make a list of the other things we still need to get."

Out of sight around the corner from the lobby, Isabel slapped her hand across her mouth to keep from bursting into laughter. With her other hand, she squeezed her stomach. Yoshiko shook her head in disapproval but grinned at the same time. Frank was bent over the desk, thinking about the list.

"I shouldn't let you talk me into these things," Yoshiko whispered. "I get nervous just watching them." She peeked her head around the corner at the two boys.

"This is going to be so easy," Isabel whispered back. "You can't tell me you don't have fun with me."

"If it's so much fun, why do I feel so guilty?" Yoshiko watched as her own brother stood next to Frank. Kaneko had entered into Frank's project as fully as Frank himself.

Frank laid a piece of paper on Mr. Wakamutsu's desk and began his list. "We'll ask Mrs. Watson to make more cookies, and Mama has some leftover candy from New Year's." He wrote down *cookies* and *candy*.

"We can't give them all sweets," Kaneko said.

"But they deserve a treat every once in a while."

"I think we should give them some soap bars," Kaneko suggested. "Then they can get ready for the clean clothes."

"Good idea." Frank wrote down *soap*. "Maybe some of the people in the building have some old towels, too."

"And blankets," Kaneko said.

Frank wrote down every idea. He would decide later which ones were most important.

Isabel stifled her giggles, straightened her dress, and stepped out into view. She walked casually across the lobby.

"Hello, Frank."

He glanced up. "Hello, Isabel."

"What are you doing?"

"Just checking supplies." He stuck the end of the pencil in his mouth and blinked his eyes.

"Do you have everything you need?" Isabel asked earnestly.

Frank pursed his lips and looked at the list. "We need a few more things. But I think we will be able to get them."

"Then what's wrong?" Isabel asked.

"Some things are missing."

"Missing?" Isabel sounded genuinely puzzled.

Yoshiko poked Isabel in the ribs from behind. Isabel held her face straight.

"I'm sure I put more things in this cabinet Mr. Wakamutsu gave me, but I can't find them."

"Oh. I'm sure they'll turn up." Isabel opened her fist and showed Frank the money she held in her hand. "Mama needs some things from the store. She gave me the money." She held the money out toward Frank.

"Does Mama want me to go?" he asked.

Isabel hesitated only a split second. "She would be very glad if you did."

Frank studied Isabel's face. She looked at him seriously.

"I told Mama I was going to be working down here," Frank said. "She said it was fine, as long as I was back for supper."

"Now she needs some things from the store."

"Can't you go?"

"Well, I suppose I could," Isabel said slowly. She chose her words carefully. "But the twins have been awfully busy today with one of their projects."

"So there's a big mess to clean up," Frank said.

Isabel shrugged. "You know how it is with those two."

Frank sighed. He reached out and took the money from Isabel. She almost smiled, but she swallowed hard and the urge to grin faded away.

"What does she need?" Frank asked.

"A pound of ground beef, a gallon of milk, some apples, and ten pounds of flour."

"I can't carry all that!" Frank protested.

Isabel glanced at Kaneko, who promptly said, "I'll help

you. Let me just go tell my mother I'm going."

"I'd better write this down." Frank tore off a corner of his page and made the shopping list.

Five minutes later the boys were gone, and the girls were alone in the hotel lobby. Yoshiko finally burst into laughter.

"How do you do that?" she asked.

"Do what?"

"Keep a straight face while you lie to your brother."

"I didn't lie," Isabel said. "Nothing I said was untrue."

"But you let him think he was supposed to go to the store. I heard your mother ask you to do it."

Isabel shook her head. "I never said he was supposed to go. I only said Mama needed some things and would be glad if he went—and she would be."

"I sure hope you're going to keep your New Year's resolution when this is over," Yoshiko said.

Isabel laughed. "I never made a New Year's resolution."

"Yes, you did! You promised to stop picking on Frank."

"No, I didn't."

"Well, then, you should."

"We don't have time to argue about this," Isabel said. "We have to move quickly before they come back."

"Or before my father comes in," Yoshiko added.

Isabel gasped. "I forgot about him. He comes in every afternoon to check his mail." She glanced at the big clock on the lobby wall. "It's almost time."

"I'll be on the lookout," Yoshiko said. She moved toward where the lobby opened into the hallway.

Isabel scampered out into the hall where she had left a pillow case bulging in odd shapes. With the bag clutched in both hands, she dashed back behind the desk and flung open Frank's lower cabinet. She pulled the ten missing cans of tuna out of the pillow case and stacked them neatly on the shelf.

Next to them, she set four additional cans of beans and three pair of gloves. She debated about the six tubs of toothpaste.

"Are you almost done?" Yoshiko whispered urgently. "Someone's coming."

The tap, tap, tap of footsteps across the wooden floor made Isabel's stomach tighten. She froze as she crouched behind the desk and listened. The footsteps did not sound heavy enough to be Mr. Wakamutsu, but she could not allow herself to relax. No one must see her.

"I'm looking for Isabel," a voice said.

Isabel held her breath. It was only Audrey, and she did not want her sister to see what she was doing. But she was not sure what Yoshiko would say.

Yoshiko shrugged. "You don't see her here, do you?"

"I guess not," Audrey responded. "When you see her, please tell her I'm looking for her."

"I will," Yoshiko promised.

"Tell her she has to come and help me with my book report."

"I'll tell her."

"It's due tomorrow."

"I promise, I'll tell her."

Audrey tapped away across the floor. Isabel popped up from behind the desk.

"You did that very well," she said, grinning at her friend.

"I didn't lie," Yoshiko said. She shifted her feet uncomfortably. "Audrey wants you to help with her book report. It's due tomorrow. There. Now I didn't break my promise, either."

"I'm almost done," Isabel said, ducking back down. "I'm trying to decide if I should take away something that's here."

"Just put the rest of the stuff out," Yoshiko said. "Don't forget the soap."

Isabel chuckled. "Look, he's got soap on his list." She picked up the pencil and crossed out the word. Stooping down again, she neatly stacked seven bars of soap next to the beans close to the edge of the shelf.

"Quick!" Yoshiko said. "Here comes my father."

She had heard his distant footsteps just in time. Isabel darted out from behind the desk and began straightening a stack of magazines on a nearby table.

"I thought the boys were here," Mr. Wakamutsu said.

"They'll be back, Papa-san," Yoshiko said. "Kaneko went to the grocery store with Frank."

He nodded somberly and reached for his pile of mail.

The boys were soon back, both of them laden with groceries. Isabel smiled brightly at her brother and reached out for the sack he carried.

"I'll take these upstairs," she said.

Yoshiko took Kaneko's load.

With hardly a glance over their shoulders, the girls left the lobby. They nearly collapsed on the stairs in laughter. They did not go immediately upstairs. They listened carefully to the conversation that they knew would follow.

"How are the supplies?" Mr. Wakamutsu asked.

"I don't understand what's happening," Frank said as he walked around the big desk. "Some of the things that I put in here last night have disappeared."

"Disappeared?" Mr. Wakamutsu sounded alarmed. "Perhaps the maid took them."

Kaneko shook his head. "She wouldn't do that. She knows better than to go into your cupboards. Everyone does."

Mr. Wakamutsu nodded in agreement.

"But somebody must have come in here. Somebody took my things," Frank insisted. "Look, you can see for yourself." He yanked open the cabinet. The tower of soap bars tumbled off the shelf.

"Where did those come from?" Kaneko asked. "They

weren't there a few minutes ago."

"And the tuna is back!" Frank exclaimed. "And some beans. Something very strange is going on here."

On the stairs, the girls let their laughter sound free. Their giggles echoed into the lobby. Kaneko groaned and rolled his head to one side.

"Now I get it," Kaneko said.

Mr. Wakamutsu nodded, too. "The girls were here."

"That's right, Papa-san. The girls were here the whole time we were gone."

"Do you mean you think Isabel did this?" Frank asked.

"Come on, Frank, she does things like this to you all the time," Kaneko said.

Frank slammed the cupboard closed. "I didn't think she would play around with the things I'm collecting for poor people. Even Isabel is not that mean."

"It's just a prank," Kaneko said. "Don't let it upset you. After all, she didn't really hurt anything."

"I suppose Mama never said I should go to the store. After all, she gave the money to Isabel, and Isabel was right here to take the groceries up to her."

Kaneko was nodding. "See? She had it planned the whole time."

"Isabel is a good planner," Mr. Wakamutsu remarked.

Frank turned toward the stairs. "Isabel!" he called out.

Isabel and Yoshiko scrambled to their feet and dashed up the stairs.

CHAPTER 6

A Whale of a Plane

"There it is!" Isabel cried. "I can't wait to see it fly!" She leaned out over the railing on a pier that stretched out into the Puget Sound. With one hand, she pointed toward the shining metal hulk on the shoreline. Engineers and mechanics swarmed around a great aircraft, checking last minute details. Isabel was amused at their busyness and captivated at the same time. There must be a thousand things to double-check, she imagined.

"Be careful, Isabel," Frank warned. But he, too, leaned out over the railing. "Is it really going to happen, Daddy? Is the Clipper really going to fly today?"

Daddy chuckled and grinned widely. "I hope so. That's what we're here to see."

"Of course it will fly," Isabel insisted. "Why wouldn't it?"

"Don't forget that three test flights have already failed," Daddy warned her.

"Today will be the day," Isabel declared confidently. "I've waited all winter for this day to come."

"Actually you've waited two years," her father reminded her. "It was June of 1936 when Pan Am ordered six Clippers from Boeing. And now it's June of 1938."

"But you've been telling me for weeks that they were almost done. Now they really are!"

"Just the first one. A second one is still in the dock. And this one may need more work."

All through the winter and spring months, Isabel had pounced on her father every day when he came home from work. She wanted to know every detail that was happening to Boeing's Clipper. While Frank counted cans of beans and helped to wash the used clothing Daddy gathered from the men at work, Isabel concentrated on learning the names of all the parts of the Clipper. While Frank wondered what the men with no homes were going to eat for supper each night or where they were going to sleep, Isabel wondered about the future.

Mr. Wakamutsu hung all the used clothing Daddy collected on a rolling rack. Once a month, he and Daddy rolled the rack down the sidewalk to a neighborhood where they knew they would find men who needed the clothing. At first, Mama had not wanted Frank to go along. But gradually she had come to see that he was not in harm's way. Daddy made sure everyone knew that everything they did was Frank's idea. The men began to look forward to the spunky ten-year-old who brought them soap and soup and everything in between. Even Isabel helped with the collection from time to time—but only when Frank could not see her. She knew where he kept his list of supplies.

When she had something to add to the cabinet, she simply put the items on the shelves and changed the numbers on his list.

If Yoshiko was not at Japanese school after spending all day at the public school, then she was working around the hotel that her father ran. At thirteen, Yoshiko was not considered a child anymore. Her parents wanted her to work. She had always known that she would work in the family's business. So Isabel worked, too. It was the only way she could be with Yoshiko in the afternoons after they had finished their homework. Together, they cleaned the lobby, changed bedding in the guest rooms, and took careful telephone messages for Yoshiko's father.

The winter and spring had passed pleasantly. But it was the summer that Isabel looked forward to because she knew that the day would come for the Clipper to fly. She stood now with her father and Frank on a pier on Puget Sound, waiting for the Clipper to be tested once more.

"Ask me anything," Isabel said, "anything at all about the Clipper."

"How tall is it?"

Frank jumped in. "About four times as tall as Isabel."

She scowled at him, but Daddy laughed. "That's a pretty good answer. What do you say, Isabel?"

"To be precise," she said haughtily, "the hull is nineteen feet deep, divided between two decks. The upper deck is for the crew, and the lower deck is for the passengers."

"He didn't ask all that," Frank observed.

"Here's another one," Daddy said. "How many passengers can it hold?"

Frank grinned. "How many sardines can you get into a can that size?"

Isabel's glare intensified. "The Clipper will carry thirty-four passengers on flights across the ocean, and seventy-four passengers on shorter flights. Of course, that does not include the crew of ten."

"What's the wingspan?"

"One hundred and fifty feet."

"How long is the Clipper?"

"One hundred and six feet."

"How much does she weigh?"

Isabel hesitated only a second. "She weighs just over eighty-two thousand pounds."

"How fast does the Clipper go?" Daddy asked.

"I know this one," Frank interjected. "She can go 193 miles per hour."

Isabel squinted her eyes and looked at Frank. "Where did you learn that?"

"The Clipper is practically the only thing you talk about anymore," Frank answered. "When you say something enough times, I remember it."

"Do you have any idea how fast 193 miles per hour is?" Isabel quizzed her brother.

"About as fast as you run when I catch on to one of your tricks."

"What tricks?" Isabel asked innocently.

Frank groaned and took a boxer's stance. He boxed at the air in front of Isabel.

"Take it easy, Frank," Daddy said. "You know how your mother feels about boxing."

"But it's fun," Frank insisted. "It's a game, just like any other game."

"Except people get hurt in boxing," Isabel said. "That's why Mama doesn't like it."

"I don't want to be a boxer," Frank said, "I just want to see a real fight some day—just once." He hooked his left fist under an imaginary chin and came in hard with his right.

"Don't get your heart set on it, Son. Your mother will never agree to it."

"I can keep hoping, can't I?"

"Ask me about the engine, Daddy," Isabel pleaded, not at all interested in debating the boxing question any further.

"What kind of engine is in the 314 Clipper?"

"It has four engines. They are fifteen hundred horsepower Wright GR-2600 twin cyclone engines."

"Very good." Daddy nodded. "How high can it fly?"

"The highest it can go is sixteen thousand feet."

"And how far?"

"It can go almost five thousand miles."

"Why do you need to know all that stuff?" Frank asked.

"Someday I'll fly a plane," Isabel said. "You can never know too much about the plane that you're flying."

"That's a good attitude, Isabel," Daddy said.

"I think I see something," Frank said. "It's much closer now."

"This is it," Daddy agreed. "It won't be long now, Isabel."

"Thank you for bringing me down here," she said. "If the other test flights had worked, I wouldn't get to see this one."

Daddy smiled. "I guess that's true."

"What happened on the other ones?" Frank asked.

"There were several problems," Daddy explained. "The first time, all fifty-six spark plugs had gone bad and had to be changed. The second time, a gust of wind tipped the plane, and the starboard wing almost went under the water. The plane was too light. We had to add more sandbag ballast."

"Then did it fly?"

Daddy shook his head. "The next time, the copilot made an error and nearly tipped the plane over again. Everyone is still getting used to the power that comes from the new 100-octane fuel."

"But it's going to fly today!" Isabel said, her dark eyes glowing with excitement. "Pretty soon, we'll be able to go to Europe in a plane that you helped to build, Daddy."

"Europe!" Daddy exclaimed. "That would be quite an adventure."

"Sure. We'll sit in the lounge all day, reading and playing games. When it's lunchtime, we'll go to the dining salon. The crew will bring out the white tablecloths and the fancy food."

"What about when it's bedtime?" Frank wanted to know.

"Then we'll go to bed, silly," Isabel said. "The crew will fix our berths, just like they do on a train."

"I've never been on a train," Frank said, "and neither have you."

"You can imagine, can't you?"

"It looks like a whale!" Frank exclaimed.

Isabel stretched her neck. The plane was in full view as it eased into the water.

"It's enormous!" Isabel said, her eyes wide. "I've never seen anything so huge in my whole life."

Frank scoffed. "You were the one bragging that you knew all the specifications."

"Yes, but when you see it up close, it's so big!"

"One of the biggest planes ever built," Daddy said.

"Look at those windows," Isabel said. "You could look down on the whole world from sixteen thousand feet up in the air."

"Everything would look like ants," Frank said.

"I wouldn't care."

"I see the pilot," Frank said.

"That's Eddie Allen," Daddy remarked. "He's one of the best there are. If he can't fly this thing, no one can."

A moment later, the engines rumbled, and the propellers on the four twin engines began to spin. The ground crew scurried to get out of the way.

"What's he waiting for?" Frank asked.

"He wants the engines to be warmed up," Isabel said.

A few minutes later, the pilot was ready to go. He gave the ready sign through the window, and the plane began to move forward.

Frank covered his ears at the thundering engines in full gear. The whale of a plane moved out over the water and lifted into the air. Daddy, Isabel, and Frank held on to the railing and tilted their heads back to watch.

"It's like looking at the belly of a big fish," Frank shouted.

The plane leaned first to one side, then the other. Finally it straightened out and headed in a direct line along its path.

"When will it come back?" Frank asked.

"It won't," Daddy said. "It's going to land on Lake Washington. When I get to work tomorrow, I'll find out what Eddie has to say about it. I'm sure we'll have some work to do."

"That was beautiful," Isabel exclaimed, breathless.

Daddy smiled. "This is the beginning of a whole new era of air travel," he said. "More and more people are going to go by air from now on."

"I know I want to," Isabel said.

"What happened to the planes you used to work on?" Frank asked.

"Those were for the army," Daddy said. "They wanted bombers that could fly across the ocean."

"Is there going to be a war?" Frank wanted to know.

A shadow passed over Daddy's face. "Frank, I wish I could promise that there would be no war. But I can't. The planes that I worked on might carry bombs to Europe instead of carrying passengers."

"I'm not going to think about that!" Isabel asserted. "Please, Daddy, can't we go to Lake Washington and see the plane come down?"

CHAPTER 7

Adventure on the Mountain

"How come we didn't get a cobertible?" Barbara asked. She wiped sweat from her face with a pudgy fist.

"A cobertible?" Daddy asked. As he drove, he glanced over his shoulder at his youngest daughter in the center of the back seat.

"I think she means convertible," Mama said.

"I want a cobertible so we won't be so hot," Barbara said.

"Me, too," Ed agreed.

Daddy checked to see that his window was rolled down as far as it would go. "I know it's hot. That's why we're going to the mountain. It will be much cooler on the mountain."

"But I don't want to get wet," Ed said.

Daddy was puzzled. "Why would you get wet? There's not a cloud in the sky."

"You said the mountain is rainier."

"I did?"

Mama started laughing. "Eddie, the mountain is called Mt. Rainier, but it's not going to rain."

Ed sat back, satisfied. "Good. I don't like the rain."

"But I still want a cobertible," Barbara said insistently.

"Convertible," Isabel said, sighing. With five children squeezed into the back seat, there was no room to move her arms. Frank's elbow was planted in her ribs on one side. On the other, she was boxed in by Barbara pressed up against her thigh. Eddie was next, and Audrey had the spot next to the window.

The Harringtons hardly went anywhere together in a car. Most cars simply were not made to carry nine people at one time. They had come across the country from Minneapolis in a 1925 Chrysler, but they had all been smaller then. Ed and Barbara were hardly more than babies three years ago. Now they were squirmy four-year-olds who took up a lot more room.

A few months earlier, Daddy had sold the Chrysler and bought a 1932 Ford V-8. It had more power, he said, and they would need the extra power if they were going to explore the mountains around Seattle.

At least Steven and Alice had not come along on this exploration. That gave the rest of them a little bit more room than they usually had.

"I'm hot, Daddy." Audrey added to the chaos in the car with her own declaration of the heat. "Why does it have to be so hot?"

"It's been a hot summer," Daddy answered. "We just have to make the best of it."

Mama turned around in the front seat and smiled at her five youngest children lined up in the back seat. "It's going to be so much cooler when you can get out and run around Mt. Rainier."

"You keep saying that," Audrey whined, "but it's taking a long time to get there."

"I'm boiling!" Barbara said emphatically.

"I'm boiling," Eddie echoed.

Isabel rolled her eyes in frustration, but she had to agree with the twins. If she did not get out of the hot car soon, maybe her blood would start to boil. Even with all the windows open, it was like riding around inside a furnace.

"I've wondered about this mountain for so long," Isabel said. "I can see it all the way from Seattle when the weather is clear. I'm glad somebody finally decided that people ought to be allowed to climb it."

Daddy pushed his dark eyebrows together. "Don't get any ideas, Isabel. We're not really going to climb the mountain. We're just going to stroll along a few trails and try to stay cool. It shouldn't be much longer now." He steered the car off the main road onto a side road. Everyone fell silent as they watched the terrain begin to rise and give way to a shady, thick forest.

A few minutes later, Daddy parked the car at the base of the mountain.

"I don't see the mountain," Audrey said.

"You can't see it when you're close up," Frank said.

"Then how do you know it's here?"

"You're already on it," Frank informed her.

Mama chuckled. "Just wait until you get out and walk around. It will feel like a mountain."

"Everybody out!" Daddy said cheerfully. He opened his door and got out. The children tumbled out after him.

"That's a relief," Isabel said, and she unbent her tall frame and stood next to the car. "I feel cooler already."

"Barbara, where are you going?" Mama called.

"To climb the mountain," came the reply.

Mama scurried after the twins. "You two have to wait for the rest of us." Barbara pouted, but she turned around and slowly walked back toward the family. She refused to let Mama hold her hand.

"We need a few ground rules," Daddy said. "We stay together at all times."

"But Daddy," Isabel protested, "we've been squished in that car for a long ride. What's the point of coming to see the mountain if we have to stay squished together?"

Daddy sighed. "I just don't want anyone to get lost. You and Frank can go ahead a little ways, but don't go so far ahead that we can't see you. Do you understand?"

Frank and Isabel nodded. Together, the seven Harringtons turned toward the path that would begin their hike up the mountain.

"I want to see the glaciers, Daddy," Frank said. "I read about them in that book you gave me."

"I thought the glaciers were in Alaska," Audrey said.

"Most of them are," Daddy explained. "That's what makes Mt. Rainier so remarkable. It has several glaciers."

"I want to get as close to one as I can," Frank said.

Daddy consulted a pamphlet he had in his hand. "I think we are on the right side of the mountain to see the glaciers. You just have to be patient while we walk for a while."

"What's a glacier?" Eddie asked.

"It's a huge, enormous, tremendous block of ice that has been frozen since long before it was ever discovered by people," Frank explained.

"Why doesn't it melt?" Ed asked.

"Because it's so cold, freezing cold, and so big that even the sun doesn't melt it."

"I don't get it," Audrey said. "The sun can melt anything."

"Not this glacier," Frank said. "Just wait and see. It's part of the mountain."

"I see it!" Isabel said.

"Where?" Frank asked eagerly. His eyes scanned the horizon. "Where is the glacier?"

"Oops," Isabel said. "I guess it was just a reflection in the sunlight." She forced her lips not to smile as she watched Frank anxiously searching for the glacier.

"You're right!" Frank said excitedly, pointing. "Look! It's beautiful!"

Surprised, Isabel lifted her eyes once more. Sure enough, a glacier sparkled in the sunlight on the rocky mountainside. Its brightness looked like glare from the sun, and it took a moment for her to focus her eyes.

"I thought it would be snowy," Isabel said. "But it's ice, pure ice."

Frank was transfixed. "I've never seen anything so spectacular in all my life."

"Then let's get going," Daddy urged. And they began to walk again.

They came to a meadow. Mama stopped and took a deep breath.

"Do you smell those wildflowers?" she asked everyone. "Donald, we've spent too much of our lives living in big cities. Look at the gorgeous flowers."

The scene before them reminded Isabel of a painting. Sprigs of blue and yellow and pink blurred together across the green landscape. The more closely she looked, the more variety of flowers she saw. Somehow she had always thought that wildflowers ought to look wild and ferocious and overgrown.

But these were delicate and tender. And no meadow ever smelled as sweet as that sloping spring meadow on the side of a mountain.

"Come on, Frank," Isabel said. "Let's run."

"But Daddy said to stay together."

"He said you and I could go ahead a little ways. We won't be out of their sight," Isabel said. "They can see us across the meadow."

"We should stay here."

"But I think we're getting closer to the glacier," Isabel said. "You don't want to miss that."

"Where? Show me!"

Isabel pointed vaguely across the meadow. "Over there."

Frank glanced over his shoulder. "Well, I suppose it's all right as long as they can see us." He fell into step with Isabel. Running was not as easy as she thought it would be. The slope of the mountain made it difficult to run uphill. And the wild grasses and weeds in some places were up to their waists. Together, they tromped across the meadow as efficiently as they could.

"I guess that wasn't the glacier after all," Isabel said after a few minutes.

Frank stopped and put his hands on his hips. He glared at Isabel. "Is this another one of your silly tricks?"

Isabel laughed aloud. "Maybe it is, maybe it isn't."

"We should wait for the others," Frank said.

"They can still see us," Isabel said. But she did not turn around to look.

"I don't see them," Frank said.

"That doesn't matter, as long as they can see us." Isabel charged ahead. "It feels so good to get out and move around as much as we want to."

Frank glanced over his shoulder. He could not see the rest

of his family, and he certainly did not want to lose sight of Isabel. Reluctantly he followed the path she'd made in the high grass.

"Look, the glacier!" Isabel said.

"I'm not falling for that again," Frank said.

"No, I mean it. I see the glacier!"

"Stop it, Isabel. Let's turn around and find the others."

Isabel reached out and grabbed Frank's arm. She tugged him in front of her and put her hands firmly on his shoulders. "Look, there. Do you see it?"

In Isabel's grip, Frank had no choice but to look at where she pointed. His eye caught an icy gleam sparkling in the sunlight. Slowly he took a few steps closer and swept his eyes up the mountainside. The thick white ice before him rose majestically, sparkling brilliantly in the bright day.

"Wow!" Frank said softly. "It really is the glacier."

"Of course it is, silly," Isabel said. "Isn't that what you were looking for?"

"It's so close, so real. I can't even imagine how something could be that way for so many years," Frank said. "Look at everything growing around it. But the glacier stays there. It's like time is standing still."

Isabel lowered her voice and put her head close to Frank's. "I've heard of people wandering the mountain for years," she said. "Hermits come up here to get away from all the people in the city. Then they get lost and can't find their way out. They wander around for years until they finally go insane."

Frank pulled back and looked at his sister. "You're making that up."

"You can believe me or not," Isabel said, shrugging her shoulders. "I'm just telling you what I've heard."

Frank turned back toward the glacier. "It's an incredible part of nature. I suppose sometimes a little of it melts on the surface, but it probably just freezes over again. I wonder what it's like on the inside."

"I'm sure you would find all sorts of interesting things inside," Isabel said seriously.

"Like what?"

"Like bodies," Isabel answered confidently, "of people who lived in caves and got caught in a river that froze. Things like that."

"There aren't any people in the glacier," Frank said cautiously.

"How do you know?" Isabel challenged him. "Has anyone really seen the center of a glacier?"

"Scientists must know about it," Frank said.

"I'm telling you what some scientists think," Isabel insisted.

"I never heard that before."

"You haven't read as much as I have," Isabel answered.

Frank looked at his sister and then at the glacier. Suddenly he wanted to be with the rest of the family and not in this meadow alone with Isabel.

"We should go tell the others we found the glacier," Frank said.

"You go if you want to," Isabel said.

Frank turned around. The sea of grass around them looked identical in every direction. The path that they had made was nowhere to be seen.

"Isabel, I think we're lost," Frank admitted.

"Don't be silly." Isabel turned and began to trudge back across the meadow. "This is the way we came."

Frank followed her. He wanted to believe that she knew where she was going. But nothing looked familiar. He put his hand up to shade his eyes and peered down the hill as they walked. Surely by now he ought to catch a glimpse of Audrey's red jumper or Mama chasing the twins. But he saw only an endless meadow.

"Isabel," he said cautiously, "do you know where you're going?"

"Down the mountain, of course."

"I don't think we came this way," Frank said. "It doesn't look right."

"It has to be. We came straight up from the road."

Frank shook his head. "I don't think we walked very straight."

Isabel stopped and sighed. The last thing she wanted to do was admit that Frank was right. But she felt completely topsy-turvy and hardly knew up from down. She had no idea which way to go to find her family.

"We're lost, aren't we, Isabel?" Frank said.

Slowly she nodded.

CHAPTER 8
Lost!

"I think we should go this way," Isabel announced. She veered to the left and tromped through the grass as if she knew exactly where she was going. Her knees stepped high to keep from getting tangled up in the wildflowers, but she kept her pace quick and determined.

Frank sneezed. "I think I'm allergic to all these flowers and grass." He sneezed again. More slowly, he followed in Isabel's footsteps.

"We can't do anything about that," Isabel said. "You'll just have to make do until we find Mama."

He sneezed again, three times. "That's easy for you to say. I need a handkerchief."

"Under the circumstances, I think Mama would let you use your sleeve. Just follow me."

"I thought you said you were lost." Frank awkwardly wiped his nose against his own shoulder.

"It's a temporary condition," Isabel said. "I'll figure out where we are before too long."

"Are you sure?"

"Of course. We didn't come very far. We just have to find that path we started out on. It's around here somewhere."

"It's been a long time since we saw anyone," Frank said. He was getting tired of the effort it took to move around on the mountainside. And it was getting hard for him to breathe. "I wish I had a watch."

"It's only been a few minutes," Isabel insisted. "Not more than ten."

"It seems like a lot longer." Frank sneezed again. He was sure much more than ten minutes had passed since they had seen their parents. Frank stopped and turned around to look behind them at the glacier. It still glinted in the late afternoon sun. Frank studied the rock formations on both sides of the great slab of ice. He wanted something to be familiar. They had not done a very good job of finding their bearings up until now. Focusing on the glacier, they had paid no attention to the details of their surroundings. They would have to do better if they were going to find their parents.

"Come on, slowpoke," Isabel said. "Do you want to get out of here or not?"

Frank did not move his feet. Following Isabel had gotten him into this mess, and he did not want things to get any worse. "I don't think you know where you're going," he said to the back of her head.

"Trust me. I'm your big sister."

"But you don't know anything about Mt. Rainier."

Isabel finally stopped and looked at Frank. She put her hands on her hips in exasperation. "You don't know any more than I do. Somebody has to be in charge. It might as well be me." Confidently, Isabel began to walk faster.

Frank followed, but he did not watch Isabel. Instead, he studied their surroundings. He took notice of the bluebird hydrangea growing in clumps and the purple lupine growing thin and tall in a straight line up the mountainside. The whole meadow had looked the same when they first came upon it— splashes of color accenting the sloping field of willowy grass. He had not noticed any pattern to the way the wildflowers grew. Now, of course, it mattered where they were in the meadow. Frank wished he had paid more attention during the walk in. He forced himself to look at the field until he began to see distinct landmarks.

"Are you coming or not?" Isabel called over her shoulder. She seemed determined to blaze the trail whether she knew where she was going or not.

"Isabel, wait," Frank said. He sneezed again several times.

"Just keep up."

"No, stop. I don't think this is right."

"How would you know?"

"Isabel, please stop," Frank pleaded.

Exasperated, Isabel stopped and turned around to see what was on Frank's mind.

"We're walking uphill," Frank said, "and it's getting steeper."

"It's a mountain. Of course we're walking uphill."

"But Isabel, we walked uphill when we first came to the meadow. We walked uphill to find the glacier. If we want to go back, shouldn't we walk downhill?"

Isabel had to admit Frank had a point. But she did not want to admit it to him. "A mountain has lots of ups and downs."

"Isabel, be sensible."

"I am being sensible. We have to keep moving to find our way out of here."

Frank shook his head slowly and wiped his nose once more. "I think we should stay put. Nobody will ever find us if we keep moving."

"Nobody has to find us. We'll find them."

"I don't think so."

"Frank Harrington, you listen to me!" Isabel shook her finger at her brother. "We're not going to just stay here and do nothing. We're going to find our way out."

Frank put his hands on his hips and faced Isabel squarely. "I'm not going with you, Isabel. I'm going back to where we saw the glacier while I can still find it." He turned around and began to retrace his steps. Frank refused to look over his shoulder to see what Isabel was doing, but his heart pounded. If she insisted on going in another direction and they got separated, what would he do then?

"I suppose you know that the bears like the glacier," Isabel said.

"What bears?" Frank asked. He didn't turn around, but he did slow his steps.

"The bears that live on the mountain, of course. They stay close to the ice."

"You're making that up." He speeded up again. He was not going to fall for one of Isabel's tricks in a serious situation like this.

"Suit yourself."

Isabel did not say anything else, but she did begin to follow Frank. The land was sloping downhill again, which made Frank feel better. The mountain meadow swirled around them. Frank's eyes swept the horizon, looking for any sign of the rest of their family.

"Mama's going to be mad," he said softly. "Daddy told

us not to wander off."

Isabel nodded somberly. Then she rose to her own defense. "We didn't wander off. They just didn't keep up."

"I don't think Mama will see it that way." Frank stopped. "This is the part of the glacier that we first found. I think we should wait here for a while. We're out in plain view, and we can see anyone who might come along."

Isabel plopped to the ground. "It's cooler here than in Seattle, but it's still hot."

Still scanning the horizon, Frank slowly lowered himself to the ground next to Isabel.

"Mama said we were going to have a picnic supper," Isabel said. "I'm ready for it right now."

"You have to find Mama before you can eat," Frank said.

"I know that. But we're not going to find her sitting here. I still think we should keep looking for that path."

"Maybe," Frank said reluctantly. "But we have to make sure we don't start wandering around in circles. We need landmarks. And we need to pay attention to the sun."

Isabel looked at her brother with her eyebrows raised in surprise. "Sometimes you have good ideas." She tilted her head back and looked at the sun. "It's getting lower in the sky, so that way must be west."

"Which side of the mountain did we come in on?" Frank asked.

Isabel shrugged. "I was going to look at Daddy's pamphlet, but I never did."

"I hope he still has it. Maybe it will help him find us."

"I don't think we actually went all the way around the mountain," Isabel said convincingly. "That would be miles and miles of hiking."

"Then we're still on the same side we came in on. That's good."

"I can't just sit here, Frank," Isabel exclaimed, springing to her feet. "We can't just sit here and wait for Daddy to find us. We have to keep looking."

Frank turned his head in both directions. "All right. But we'll keep coming back to this spot. We won't go so far away that we can't get back to this part of the glacier. Do we have a deal?"

Reluctantly Isabel nodded. "We have a deal."

They walked for about fifteen minutes down the mountain.

"Does anything look familiar?" Frank asked several times.

Each time Isabel shook her head. They returned to their spot near the glacier and waited some more. Then Isabel chose another direction and they hiked again. All afternoon they did this. The sun began to cast its long shadow across the meadow.

"It's getting cooler," Isabel said. "I wish I had a sweater."

"I have a feeling it's going to get a lot colder," Frank responded. "We should start looking for shelter."

"Shelter! I have no intention of spending the night on this mountain." Isabel was adamant.

"Isabel, don't get crazy. It's going to be dark soon, and we haven't found the path."

"We can't give up."

"We're not giving up," Frank said. "We're just being sensible. Mama would want us to be sensible."

"I suppose you're right. We have to find shelter." Isabel made the statement as if it were her idea. "There," she said, pointing. "We can stay under those trees."

"I saw a rock," Frank said. "It was hollowed out on the inside, like a small cave. It was pretty deep. We'd have more protection there."

"Protection from what?" Isabel asked. "I was just teasing about the bears."

"But there might be wind or even rain. We could sit under

the rock, but we would still be able to see out if anyone came looking for us."

The sun was fading quickly from the sky. It would be only a few more minutes before darkness enfolded them.

"Do you think they're still looking for us?" Frank asked.

Isabel nodded vigorously. "Daddy would never give up."

"But he might wait until morning for the light," Frank said. "Otherwise, he might get lost, too."

Isabel sighed. "Show me the rock."

They climbed until they were quite close to the glacier.

"It was right along here," Frank said thoughtfully, his eyes searching the landscape. He led the way, and Isabel followed. "Here it is."

Isabel stooped in front of the hollowed rock. She ran her fingers along the cold surface. "It's so smooth. Maybe the glacier carved out this little cave."

"It makes me think of that song Mama sings," Frank said.

"What song?"

"I don't remember all the words," Frank said, thinking hard. "It's something about how God hides our souls in the cleft of the rock. Mama says it means God keeps us safe."

"I think that's a Bible verse," Isabel said. "I remember learning it in Sunday school. He hides us in the cleft of the rock and covers us with His hand."

"Do you believe it?"

"Believe what?"

"That God will keep us safe," Frank said. "He gave us a rock."

"And we're always in His hands," Isabel added.

"Maybe we should pray," Frank suggested.

Isabel nodded slowly. "We should have thought of that a long time ago. I thought I could find the way out by myself."

"I've never prayed for something like this before," Frank said. "What should we say?"

"Mama says to always be thankful when we pray," Isabel said. "We have to start with that."

"I'm thankful we haven't seen any bears," Frank said. "And I'm thankful for the hollow rock."

"Then I guess we're ready."

They squeezed their eyes shut. "Dear God," Isabel said, "thank You that we haven't seen any bears. And thank You for this rock that will give us shelter tonight. Please keep us safe. And don't let us be lost any longer than we have to be. Amen."

They opened their eyes. Gray dusk had settled around them so deeply that they could hardly see each other any longer.

"I guess we should get in there," Isabel said.

"You first," Frank urged.

Isabel did not argue. She squatted down and crawled into the hollow space. She pressed herself to one side and made room for Frank. He squirmed his way in next to her and tried to lean his head back against the rock. They sat for a long time in the silence. Around them they heard the wind rustling the high grass and crickets chirping their night song. The hooting of an owl made them both jump.

"Isabel?" Frank said softly. "I don't think I can sleep."

Isabel twisted in the tiny space and put an arm around Frank's shoulders. "We'll take turns," she said. "You lean on me for a while."

With Frank's blond head tucked against her shoulder, Isabel stared out into the darkness.

CHAPTER 9

Surprising Plans

Isabel painfully turned her head from side to side. Her neck was so stiff it cracked. She winced when she heard the sound. Her back ached all the way down her spine. Her left arm bore the weight of Frank's chest, and it was nearly numb. A million pin pricks tingled from her elbow to her wrist. Frank's head had slipped off her shoulder hours ago, and her own head had fallen back against the hard rock.

Somehow the tiny cave had seemed bigger when they first crawled into it. Huddling together had made them feel safer. Isabel's knees were drawn tightly up against her chest right under her chin. As she gradually awoke, she realized how badly she wanted to stretch them out. Her knees screamed for release.

Frank was still asleep. The expression on his face was far too peaceful, considering their circumstances. His blond hair fanned across his forehead, above his closed eyes. Long, delicate eyelashes brushed his cheeks. He looked as peaceful as if he were sleeping in his own bed at home.

Isabel was surprised that she had fallen asleep at all. After they'd crawled under the shelter of the rock, darkness had settled around them quickly. They had huddled together and stared into the darkness, not knowing what might be out there. The crickets' concert was comforting at first.

But later in the night, the howling had started. Frank had begun to believe that maybe there were bears outside the cave. Isabel could not decide if she was hearing the harmless hoot of a distant owl or the cry of a hungry wolf. Whatever it was, she had squeezed her eyes shut and prayed for it to stop. And soon it had. But her heart beat rapidly for a long time after that— long after Frank had surrendered to sleep.

The temperature dropped swiftly after dark, making Isabel shiver as she sat awake in the dark. She was glad for the warmth of Frank next to her. Eventually, though, even Isabel gave in to her exhaustion and slept. And now she had awakened stiff and cramped.

Isabel could see straight out of the cave. The sky before her was a pinkish gray, so Isabel knew the night would soon be over. She studied the shadows outside the cave as they took form bit by bit. Finally she was sure they were trees and rocks, not bears and wolves. Isabel was determined to leave the little cave as soon as she could see more than ten yards in front of her face. Gently she nudged Frank's weight off of her left arm. He stirred and moaned slightly.

"Frank," Isabel said softly. "It's almost morning."

Reluctantly Frank opened his eyes and tried to sit up straight. "My back hurts," Frank muttered, "and I have a headache."

"You just need to stretch out," Isabel advised. "We'll both feel better when we stand up."

Frank rubbed his eyes with both hands and swallowed hard. "What are we going to do now, Isabel?"

"We're going to go back out in that meadow and try again," she answered. "Either someone will find us, or we'll find the path back to the road."

"I wish Daddy had come last night," Frank said. He rubbed the back of his neck with one hand. "I don't like sleeping in a cave."

"Well, Daddy didn't come. I don't plan to spend another night lost on this mountain, so let's get going."

"Shouldn't we wait a little longer? It's barely light out."

"It's light enough," Isabel insisted. "Mama and Daddy were probably looking for us all night, anyway."

Isabel and Frank crawled out from the small cave and stood up. They peered into the soupy gray air around them and tried to get their bearings. Inch by inch, the sky brightened. The pink hues gave way to a yellowish morning. The vivid wildflowers sprinkled around the meadow came to life once again. "Let's go this way," Isabel said, pointing.

Frank shook his head. "No, we tried that way yesterday. It wasn't right."

"We tried lots of ways yesterday. One of them has to be right."

"Isabel, I don't want to fight," Frank said. "I can hardly breathe, and my head feels like somebody drove a car over it. Can't we just sit in the meadow, at least for a while?"

"If we sit down, no one will see us in the high grass."

"Then I'll sit, and you stand." Frank sat and squinted up at his sister.

"Fine, you stay here, and I'll look for the path," Isabel said.

"No!" Frank protested. "We have to stay together."

"Oh, all right! Have it your way."

Isabel stood for a long time, scanning the horizon in every direction. The sun rose to full strength. A breeze fluttered the grass, reminding her that they had come to the mountain in search of relief from the heat. But standing in the sun, even on the mountain, got uncomfortable. Finally Isabel gave in and sat down, too. She wiped the sweat from her forehead with her arm.

"You stand for a while," Isabel said.

"I can't! My head is pounding."

"Do you want to be found, or don't you?"

"Of course I do."

"Then stand up."

Frank dragged himself to his feet with a heavy sigh. He shaded his blue eyes with his hand against his forehead and looked around. He tried to remember all the landmarks that he had found the day before. The soft colors of the wildflowers around him formed a pattern, and he concentrated on forming it in his mind.

"Hey!" Frank cried suddenly. "I see something."

Isabel sprang to her feet. "What is it?" She tried to look where he was looking.

"There!" Frank pointed. "Do you see that red spot? That must be Audrey."

Isabel did not take time to respond. She lit off down the hill at full speed. Frank stumbled down after her, groaning under his headache but determined not to be left behind.

The red spot was indeed Audrey. They kept their eyes fixed on her as they ran. By the time they reached her, Mama and Daddy and the twins were there, too, along with a man in a uniform.

Isabel hurtled herself into Daddy's arms, while Frank tumbled into Mama's.

"I assume these are your missing children," the uniformed man said with a smile.

Daddy nodded. "These are the ones. Thank you so much for your help, officer."

The man tipped his hat. "Glad to be of service. Do you folks need anything else?"

Mama shook her head. "No, we'll just go back to the car and be on our way now." She squeezed Frank so tightly he could hardly breathe.

Isabel clung to her father as they walked down the hill to the car. "I'm sorry, Daddy," she said. "It was all my fault. I should have listened to you more carefully."

Daddy squeezed her shoulder. "I'm relieved that you are all right, Isabel, and Frank, too."

"Frank found us a cave to sleep in last night," Isabel said.

"It was next to the glacier," Frank added wearily. His head throbbed with every step.

"So you found the glacier," Mama said.

"Yes, but we lost ourselves," Isabel said.

"You're safe and sound and on your way home," Mama said. "We'll talk about an appropriate punishment on the way home."

"Punishment!"

"Of course."

"But I learned my lesson," Isabel said.

"We'll just make sure you remember what you learned." Mama's voice was full of relief but firm at the same time. Isabel did not argue any more.

Several hours later Isabel emerged from the bathroom freshly bathed and wearing a clean pair of shorts with a cool white blouse. Frank had gone to bed as soon as Mama finished sponging him off. Isabel walked into the front room, where Mama was mending a hole in the knee of Eddie's favorite pants.

"Feeling better?" Mama asked.

"Yes, very much better," Isabel answered.

"Did you get enough to eat?"

"Yes. I didn't realize how hungry I was until we got home again."

"If you want something more, you can have it." Mama pursed her lips in concentration on the mending project.

"I'm sorry I wandered off, Mama," Isabel said quietly.

"You said that several times on the way home," Mama said.

"I really am sorry, truly sorry. And I'm sorry I took Frank with me. He didn't want to come, but he was afraid of getting lost if he didn't."

"He told me all about it."

"So I think the punishment is fair. I won't leave the building for two weeks."

Mama looked up from her mending. "Don't worry. You won't be lonely. Yoshiko was already here looking for you."

"Yoshiko? Can I go find her?"

"As long as you don't leave the building."

Yoshiko was in the lobby. When Isabel joined her, she reached behind the door for the extra broom she knew would be there. She fell into Yoshiko's rhythm of stretching out with the broom and pulling the dirt toward herself. Yoshiko's eyes grew wide.

"Your mother told me what happened! You must have been scared to death."

Isabel tossed her dark hair casually over her shoulder. "It wasn't so bad. I was wrong to wander off, but we were never really in any danger."

"But you were lost all night!"

Isabel shrugged her shoulders.

"Was Frank frightened?" Yoshiko asked.

"He tried to pretend he wasn't, but I could tell he was. It was a good thing I was there."

Yoshiko narrowed her eyes at her friend. "You didn't tease him, did you? You didn't try to scare him with wild stories?"

"Well, maybe just a little. But I don't think he believed me."

"He's getting smarter about you." Yoshiko swept her pile of dirt up onto a piece of cardboard and dropped it in a trash can.

"I know. He's not nearly as much fun as he used to be."

"So you were not hurt by spending a night on Mt. Rainier?"

Isabel shook her head. "Not at all."

"Rain firms the ground," Yoshiko said.

Isabel rolled her eyes. "And what does that mean?"

"Adversity builds character. When bad things happen to you, you get stronger."

The front door opened, and Yoshiko's little brothers burst into the room.

"Time to go, Yoshiko!" Abiko announced loudly.

"Go where?" Isabel wanted to know.

"We're going to see the new movie," Kaneko explained.

"*Tarzan's Revenge*? I'm dying to see that movie!" Isabel exclaimed.

"Why don't you come with us?" Yoshiko offered.

Isabel's shoulders dropped. "I'm not allowed to leave the building for two weeks."

"Two weeks! By then everybody in Seattle will have seen the movie except you," Yoshiko said, grinning.

"Don't rub it in." Isabel put the broom back behind the door. "Have a good time."

She trudged back upstairs to the Harrington apartment. Daddy had joined Mama, and they had moved to the dining room.

"Are the twins still napping?" Daddy was asking.

Mama nodded. "It was a long night for all of us. They should sleep a long time."

"And Frank?"

75

"Still has a headache. I'm hoping that he's just reacting to the trauma of being lost and that he's not getting sick again."

"I hope so, too. Perhaps when he wakes up, he'll feel fine." Daddy reached into his pocket and pulled out a folded paper. "I talked to the man at the bank again."

"And?" Mama put her mending down and gave Daddy her full attention.

"He thinks we'll be able to do it. I think we should plan to move next summer."

Isabel could not hold her questions. "Move? Move where?" she asked urgently.

Daddy turned around. "Oh, Isabel, I didn't know you were there."

"I just came in and heard you talking about moving. Are we leaving Seattle? We're not going back to Minneapolis, are we? Because I don't want to do that."

"No, no," Daddy assured her. "You've heard us talking about moving to a house of our own. I think we might be ready to do that very soon."

"Really? A house of our own?"

Mama smiled and nodded. "Next summer. We should be able to manage the down payment by then."

A cloud passed over Isabel's face. "A house would be nice, but what about the Wakamutsus? I don't want to leave them."

Mama glanced at Daddy. "We've talked about that. We won't move far. You'll still be able to see Yoshiko as much as you want to."

"Wow! A house of our own. No more carrying groceries up the stairs. No more loud radios at the neighbors' place. I'd like to live in a house again."

"So would I," Mama agreed. "But don't tell the others just yet. Let's wait until we're absolutely sure it's going to happen."

Isabel grinned. "My lips are sealed."

CHAPTER 10
The Fight

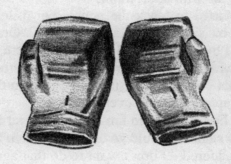

"Are you going to do it?" Kaneko's black eyes squinted at Frank. His lower lip twitched nervously.

Frank shrugged. "Maybe." He plunged his hands into his pockets and looked away as he dragged his left foot through the dusty ground in front of the apartment building.

"You have to decide," Kaneko prodded.

"I suppose the guys will want to know."

"Is everybody going?" Kaneko asked.

"Lots of guys are, and I will if you will. Will you?"

"I will if you will," Kaneko declared.

"So you're going?"

"If you're going." Kaneko raised his fists to playfully box at the air around Frank.

Frank returned the gesture. "We could take on those professional boxers any day." He came in with his left fist under Kaneko's chin and stopped just short of hitting it. Kaneko swung his right fist at Frank's stomach.

"Can you imagine seeing Al Hostak fight Freddie Steele?" Kaneko asked. "I asked my father if we could get tickets for the fight tonight, but he wouldn't even think about it."

"I didn't dare ask," Frank said. "I know Mama would say no. She says no to everything that has to do with boxing." He swiped at the air with a left hook.

Kaneko started to block the punch, but instead he put his arms down at his sides. "It's too hot," he said. "Our apartment is like an oven. I thought it would be better out here, but it's not."

"I know what you mean." Frank sat on the stoop and wiped sweat from his forehead. "At least you live on the first floor. The upstairs apartments are even hotter."

"I wish I had a big huge fan that I could sit in front of all day," Kaneko said, "or could go to the mountain like you did."

Frank shuddered. "I don't want to do that again for a very long time."

"Just leave Isabel at home the next time," Kaneko advised.

"She didn't mean any harm," Frank said.

"Don't be too sure," Kaneko responded.

Frank did not want to talk about Mt. Rainier. "Maybe we could get a fire hydrant open," he suggested.

"The fire department wouldn't like that."

"But until they got here, we could get cooled off."

"Look over there at Mrs. Mori," Kaneko said, pointing. "I've never seen her sitting out on her stoop before."

"You're right. She must be really hot."

"And down there Mrs. Swenson has a bucket of water for her baby to play in."

"I could use a bucket of water," Frank said. He wiped his

78

face again. "It's been so hot all summer. This is only July 26. It could be hot like this for weeks."

"I hope not," Kaneko said. "I suppose the ring will be really hot tonight, too."

"A little heat won't make any difference to guys like Al Hostak and Freddie Steele."

"But it will be hot for everyone watching," Kaneko said. He sat next to his friend. "Are you really going to go?"

"I will if you will," Frank countered.

"I'm not sure how we could do it," Kaneko said. "How can we get away without our parents catching us, much less get all the way downtown and sneak into the fight?"

Frank shrugged one shoulder. "I'm not worried about that. Some of the other boys have snuck into baseball games before. If they can do it, we can do it. We'll figure it out."

"So you think we should?"

"I sure think we could," Frank answered.

"So you are going?"

"If you are. Are you?"

Kaneko nodded. "So how will we do it?"

"You worry a lot, Kaneko," Frank said. "And you ask too many questions. We're supposed to meet in the alley behind the building right after supper. The other guys will be there. We'll catch a streetcar and go downtown."

"I don't have any money for the streetcar."

"Don't worry about it. When we get downtown, we'll probably split up. We'll be spotted if we all try to sneak in at the same time."

"I want to stay with you," Kaneko said.

"I guess that would be all right. Two of us together would not be so suspicious."

"Uh, oh. Here come the girls." Kaneko clamped his mouth shut.

Yoshiko and Isabel approached with damp bathing suits slung over their shoulders. Their tangled wet hair still dripped onto their shoulders.

"You went swimming!" Frank exclaimed. "You've been gone all afternoon. I wondered where you went."

"We had to do something to cool off," Isabel said. "This heat is beastly. They say it's one of the worst heat spells in Seattle's history."

"Why didn't you tell us?" Kaneko asked.

"Tell you what?" Yoshiko answered.

"That you were going swimming."

"Not saying is the flower," Yoshiko said.

"Huh?" Frank scrunched up his face in confusion.

Kaneko sighed. "She means that some things are better left unsaid."

"Then why didn't she just say that?" Frank wanted to know.

"It's not the Japanese way."

"You two looked like you were talking about something very serious," Isabel said. "What's going on?"

Frank swallowed hard. "Nothing. We're just trying to keep cool, the same as you are."

"You must have been talking about something."

"We were just talking about what to do tonight."

"And what did you decide?" Isabel pressed.

Frank felt Kaneko's elbow in his side. "We, uh, we decided, that, um, we would do something together."

"That's the best you can do?" Isabel was suspicious.

"It's not any of your business," Frank said.

"Now I know something is going on," Isabel said.

"You didn't tell us you were going swimming, and we don't have to tell you where we're going."

"So you're going somewhere tonight? The two of you? Does Mama know?"

Kaneko's elbow pressed harder into Frank's rib.

Isabel laughed. "I'm sure I wouldn't be interested anyway. Come on, Yoshiko, let's go get our hair toweled dry."

When their sisters were gone, Kaneko breathed a sigh of relief. "You talk too much," he said.

"I'm sorry," Frank responded. "Sometimes I just can't help it. She tricks me into saying things I don't mean to say."

"Let's just hope she doesn't suspect anything. Now, tell me who's coming tonight."

"Butch said he would be there. He's done this lots of times. And Harry and Ira. Probably Billy Free."

"Do you think it's really okay for us to do this?"

Frank shrugged. "We're not going to hurt anybody. And we won't get hurt. It's not as if we're the ones who are going to fight."

"So you're definitely going?" Kaneko asked.

"Definitely—if you are. Are you?"

Kaneko sighed. "If you will, I will."

"Will what?" Steven's cheerful voice called out to them.

"Aw, nothin'," Frank answered. "We're just talking."

"You two want to play some baseball?" Steven asked.

"Too hot," Frank protested.

Steven lowered himself to sit on the stoop next to the younger boys. "I suppose you're right, although the Rainiers would play anyway."

"Why did they change their name?" Frank asked. "I liked it when they were the Indians."

"They got new owners and a brand new stadium," Steven said, "so I guess it makes sense that they should have a new name, too."

"But they're still the same team," Frank protested.

"It's a whole new beginning for them, now that they're playing in Sick's Stadium."

81

"That's another thing," Frank added. "That's a silly name for a baseball park."

"Get used to it. It'll be around for a long time."

The front door to the building creaked open behind them. It was Audrey.

"Mama says to come to supper," she said.

Upstairs, the Harrington kitchen was steamed up from Mama's cooking. Frank longed to take off his shirt, but he knew Mama would never let him sit at the supper table without it. The cotton fibers were plastered to his chest with his own sweat. Frank looked around the room. No one looked happy. Isabel's curly hair was even more curly. Audrey, with a book in her hand, drooped into her chair. Alice entered with one twin attached to each hand. Moisture gleamed on their faces.

Steven carried a steaming bowl of spaghetti and set it in the middle of the table. When they were all seated, Daddy gave thanks for the food.

"It's almost too hot to eat," Alice commented as she picked up the bowl of spaghetti and started to serve the twins.

"We all have to eat something," Mama said, "and drink plenty of liquid with your supper tonight."

"It'll be too hot to sleep, too," Steven said. "Even with every window open, it's suffocating to be inside."

"Someday we'll have a house again," Mama said, "and we'll have a backyard. When it gets hot like this, we'll camp out in the back at night."

"I wish we at least had a back porch," Alice said.

"Maybe we will."

"So what is everybody planning to do tonight?" Isabel asked. She stared directly at Frank. He glared back at her without speaking.

"I have a feeling the whole neighborhood will be sitting outside," Daddy said as he served himself. "That's the way it's been every night this week."

"Can we stay up late?" Barbara asked hopefully. "Can we play outside after supper?"

Mama glanced at Daddy, then said, "Yes, you can stay up late tonight. It would be cruel to try to make you sleep in this heat."

"Yippee!" In his exuberance, Eddie threw his hands in the air, knocking his plate of spaghetti to the floor. Quickly he put his hands back in his lap. "Oops."

"Whoa!" Mama said. "Let's save some excitement for Boeing's first flight across the Atlantic."

"Sorry," Eddie muttered.

"I'll help," Isabel offered as she slid out of her chair. She crawled under the table to scrape up the spaghetti. Eight pairs of legs caged her in. Quickly she found Frank's bare calf and gave it a poke with her fork.

"Ow!"

"What's that, Frank?" Mama asked.

Isabel poked her head out from under the table. "Frank, didn't I hear you saying you had some plans for tonight?"

"Oh?" Daddy asked. "Is that right?"

Frank glared at Isabel. She ducked back under the table with a wet rag to wipe up the floor.

"It's nothing, Daddy," Frank said. "Just trying to keep cool like everyone else."

"You haven't eaten much, Frank," Mama said. "Wouldn't you like more spaghetti than that?"

Frank shook his head. "Alice is right. It's too hot to eat."

"At least drink your milk," Mama asked.

Frank nodded and picked up his glass.

Isabel put a clean plate in front of Ed and filled it.

"Thank you, Isabel," Mama said. "That was thoughtful of you."

Isabel smiled sweetly and raised her eyes to meet Frank's across the table.

"Can I be excused, please?" Frank said.

"If you're sure you can't eat more," Mama said.

"I'm sure." Frank stood up and carried his plate to the sink. Steven was starting to talk about the Rainiers, so no one paid much attention as Frank crossed the kitchen, went through the front room, and left the apartment.

There was no sign of Kaneko in front of the building. Frank thought about knocking on the Wakamutsu door, but he did not want to do anything suspicious. Kaneko said he was coming, so he would come. Frank walked around the side of the building and slithered along the brick wall to the alley in the back.

"We had just about given up on you," Harry said. "Where's the Jap?"

Frank was startled that Harry referred to Kaneko as "the Jap." But he did not let his expression show his surprise.

"He said he would be here," Frank assured them. He stuck his hands in his pockets. His stomach was in a knot—the real reason he had not been able to eat any supper.

"We're not waiting much longer," Ira said firmly.

"The Japanese eat a lot of different kinds of foods at meal time," Frank said. "It takes longer to eat. He'll be here."

Frank had a funny feeling. Something was not right. It was like the times when Isabel was about to trick him.

"We'll give him three more minutes," Ira said. "Then we have to get going. We don't need him anyway. The streetcars will be packed tonight."

Frank glanced over his shoulder. Where was Kaneko? "If you don't want to wait, go ahead. We can manage on our own."

"You're not chickening out, are you?" Harry asked.

Frank licked his dry lips.

CHAPTER 11
The Emergency

Frank glanced over his shoulder at the apartment building. Where was Kaneko? He looked back at Harry and Ira.

"He'll be here," Frank insisted.

"It's been long enough," Harry said. He kicked up a swirl of dry dirt. "We have to go."

Harry and Ira turned to walk away.

"Are you coming?" Ira asked.

"I'm going to wait for Kaneko. He won't know how to get in by himself."

"It's just as well," Harry said. "Having a Jap with us just makes us look suspicious."

"No, it doesn't," Frank protested. He hated the way Harry

talked about Kaneko. "Besides, why should we look suspicious? I thought you've done this before."

Ira laughed. "Just admit it, Frank. You're too chicken to come."

Frank could think of nothing to say. He watched as Harry and Ira and Butch strolled confidently down the alley, turned the corner around the building, and headed for the street. They gave him one last haughty look before they disappeared from sight.

Frank scowled at the evening sky. Kaneko was not coming, and Frank had used Kaneko as an excuse not to go, either. He wanted to see that fight! He had never seen a professional boxing match. To see a championship fight between Freddie Steele and Al Hostak would be an incredible experience. How could he pass it up?

Maybe he was a chicken after all. Now he would have to listen to the other boys tell all about it as they reminded him that he stayed behind. He was starting to get a headache just thinking about it.

As he put his hand to his forehead, Frank heard footsteps behind him. He wheeled around, saying, "It's about time!"

He was expecting Kaneko. But instead it was Isabel.

"Time for what?" she asked, with a bit of a sneer on her lips.

"Never mind," Frank muttered.

"I saw your buddies walking toward the streetcar stop," Isabel informed him.

"They're not my buddies."

"Oh? It was Harry and Butch and Ira—those boys that you're always pretending to box with. You know, the boys that Mama doesn't really like very much."

"There's nothing wrong with them."

"So you admit they are your friends!"

Frank glared at his sister. "I'm not in the mood for this, Isabel."

He started to leave the alley. She followed him.

"Are they sneaking into the big fight tonight?" Isabel asked. "Is that what you and Kaneko were planning to do?"

Frank let his shoulders sag. There was no point in trying to hide anything from Isabel. She had everything figured out. He said, "Kaneko didn't show up."

"I'm glad one of you showed some good sense. Mama would have a fit."

"Don't tell Mama about this, Isabel," Frank pleaded. "After all, I didn't really do anything."

"But you thought about it."

"You do crazy stuff all the time, and you never get into trouble." They started to walk back toward the apartment.

"Have you already forgotten that night on the mountain?" Isabel responded. "I learned my lesson. Sometimes parents know what they're talking about."

"Mama doesn't understand that boxing is just a sport," Frank said as they turned the corner and came around the front of the building. "It's just a contest to see who is better."

"Mama loves games," Isabel reminded Frank, "but she doesn't like to see people getting hurt. She saw enough of that when she was younger."

"It's not the same kind of fighting," Frank insisted.

"It sure looks the same to me."

"So you agree with Mama?"

Isabel nodded. "I don't understand why grown men would want to beat each other up and call it a sport."

"I can't think about this anymore," Frank said. "I have a headache. I have to go lie down."

"But it's way too early to go to bed—and it's too hot upstairs."

"I don't care," Frank answered wearily. "I have to lie down." He pulled open the front door of the building and began to drag himself up the steps. As Isabel watched him, a familiar feeling swept over her. The way he was walking meant only one thing. Frank was not just disappointed about missing the fight. He was getting sick again. She was sure of it.

Frank did go to bed, and he stayed there. He did not even get up to listen to the fight on the radio later that evening. He would have to wait to hear that twenty-two-year-old Al Hostak won the middleweight championship by knocking out defending champ Freddie Steele in the first minute of the first round of the fight.

When Isabel heard the news on the street, she ran up the stairs to Frank's bedroom. He seemed to be asleep, but she was sure he would want to know. She touched his bare shoulder to wake him up. Heat seared through her fingertips. Frank was burning up!

"Mama!" Isabel called as she ran back down the stairs.

Mama heard the tone in Isabel's cry and came immediately. She sat with Frank all night in the hot bedroom while his fever raged. Frank woke up for a few minutes at a time, and Mama tried to get him to take a few sips of water. Alice and Isabel took turns getting up to see if Mama needed help. They brought her fresh bowls of cool water with chips of ice in it and watched as she sponged off Frank, trying to coax the fever down.

In the morning, Frank was worse. He woke up, but he could not get comfortable. When he tried to take a deep breath, he gasped instead. Before anyone had had breakfast, Isabel was at Mama's side.

"Heat some water, Isabel," Mama instructed. "He needs steam to loosen up his breathing."

"But it's so hot in here already," Isabel said.

"Please, Isabel, just do as I ask."

Isabel scurried to the kitchen, pulled out the biggest pot she could find, filled it with water, put it on the stove, and lit the burner with a match.

Barbara came into the kitchen, dragging a bald doll behind her. "What are you doing?"

"Boiling water," Isabel answered absently.

"I'm not having boiled water for breakfast!" Barbara said with disapproval.

"It's not for you. It's for Frank."

"Frank doesn't want boiled water for breakfast, either."

"He's not going to eat it. He's going to breathe it."

"Only fish can breathe in water."

Isabel sighed. "Frank is sick, Barbara. Mama wants some hot water so Frank can breathe the steam."

Barbie climbed up into a chair at the table. "Why does Frank get sick so much?"

"I don't know," Isabel mumbled, "he just does. When it happens, we all have to help."

"But you don't like Frank."

"Of course I like Frank. Why would you say such a thing?"

"Because you always tease him and play tricks on him," Barb answered.

"He knows it's just for fun," Isabel insisted. "I'm not really hurting him."

Barbara lost interest in the conversation and changed the subject. "Are you going to make my breakfast today?"

Isabel looked around the kitchen. In a few minutes Steven and Eddie and everyone else would be coming into the room looking for breakfast. Mama would not want to leave Frank.

"I could make pancakes," Isabel said to Barb.

"Do you know how?"

"Of course I do. Mama taught me a long time ago. I'm almost fourteen years old."

Isabel stooped to a lower cupboard and removed a large glass mixing bowl. Into the bowl she put flour, buttermilk, and an egg in carefully measured amounts. She lit another burner on the stove and set the griddle on it to heat. The big pot of water was still not even bubbling around the edges.

Steven strode into the kitchen with his long, lanky legs. "How's Frank this morning?"

"Worse," Isabel answered. "Mama was up with him all night."

"I know," Steven replied. "I tried to get her to go to bed about two in the morning. I was going to sit with Frank. Daddy tried, too, but she wouldn't leave him."

"I think he's really sick this time," Isabel said sadly. "I can tell that Mama is more worried than usual. We'll have to call the doctor."

Steven sprinkled a few drops of water on the pancake griddle. It sizzled in response.

"The griddle is ready," he announced.

"Oh, the batter!" Isabel exclaimed. "I never stirred it." She picked up a spoon and frantically began to mix the pancake batter.

"I thought you said you knew how to make pancakes," Barbara sassed.

Eddie appeared in the doorway. "Pancakes! I want lots of syrup!" He climbed into a chair next to his twin.

Isabel dropped a spoonful of batter on the hot griddle. It spread into a perfect circle and quickly began to brown. She glanced at the pot and saw that the water had finally started to boil.

"You'll have to finish the pancakes, Steven," she said. "The water is hot."

"I'll take the water upstairs," Steven offered.

"No, I want to do it," Isabel said insistently. "Mama asked me to do it."

"The pot is heavy, Isabel," Steven pointed out. "Be sensible. Let me carry it upstairs and you finish the pancakes for the twins."

Without waiting for her answer, Steven grabbed two hot pads and lifted the pot by its handles. Isabel sighed.

"What's that smoke?" Barbara said, wrinkling her little nose.

Isabel whirled around and grabbed a spatula. Quickly she flipped the pancake over. It was black on one side.

"I'm not eating that!" Barbara declared.

"Me neither," Ed agreed.

Reluctantly Isabel had to admit that the pancake was burned. She scooped it up with the spatula and dropped it in the trash.

"We'll try again," she said.

"Pay attention this time," Barbara warned sternly, her four-year-old eyes narrowed at Isabel.

The clock ticked so slowly it seemed that time had come to a stop. But finally Isabel had managed to cook two pancakes for each of the twins, smother them in butter and syrup, and place them, still steaming, in front of her youngest siblings.

Alice came into the kitchen in her summer bathrobe. "Have you noticed it's not so hot this morning?" she asked Isabel. "I think the heat is breaking."

Isabel held out a spatula toward her older sister. "Here, if they want more, there's plenty of batter."

"I have to get ready for work," Alice protested. "I don't have time to take care of the twins."

"I'll just be a minute," Isabel insisted. "I want to see how Frank is."

Isabel did not give Alice a chance to argue. She thrust the spatula into Alice's hand and dashed off across the apartment.

Frank was sitting up with his legs slung over the side of the bed. Mama had moved his nightstand so it was right up against the bed and covered it with a towel. The pot of steaming water was set securely on the nightstand, and another towel covered Frank's head as he bent over the pot and breathed in the steam. Daddy sat next to him on the bed, making sure Frank kept his head bent down low.

"Is it working?" Isabel asked quietly.

"It's too soon to tell," Mama answered.

"Lydia," Daddy said, "perhaps we should call the doctor."

"Not quite yet," Mama said. "First we must do all the things the doctor always tells us to do. Then we'll call."

Isabel's eyes darted from her father to her mother to her brother.

"Did you tell him about the fight?" she asked.

Daddy shook his head.

"Maybe it would cheer him up. Frank, Al Hostak knocked out Freddie Steele in the first round."

Frank's shoulders barely moved.

"I don't think the fever has dropped at all," Daddy said.

"Isabel," Mama instructed, "look in the medicine cabinet and get the rubbing alcohol the doctor gave us the last time. We'll put some on his chest."

Isabel scurried off to the bathroom to do as her mother asked. But something told her that the rubbing alcohol was not going to help, either.

CHAPTER 12

Search for a Cure

Frank was not any better all day. The rest of the Harringtons were relieved that the heat wave had finally broken. Cooler, grayer skies covered Seattle, and a refreshing breeze stirred the window curtains. The twins were not quite so cranky as they had been for the last few days. Audrey was less restless and uncomfortable. But no one could think too long about the weather while Frank was so ill.

The family took turns sponging off Frank as his temperature continued to be fiery hot. Mama boiled a pot of water three times a day, and Frank breathed in the steam. For a few minutes he seemed to breathe better.

"I need to cough, Mama," he would say, "but I can't. It hurts too much."

"You just try," Mama encouraged.

And Frank did try. Isabel winced as she stood outside his room listening to him croaking and wheezing. She even felt a little guilty for trying to fool him as much as she did. She hated the thought that he might end up in the hospital if he did not improve soon. It had been a long time since he had been this sick.

Mama rubbed Frank's back as she held a glass of water to his lips. "I can't wait for heaven," she said.

Frank looked at her in alarm. "I'm not going to die, am I?"

"Oh, no, I don't believe so," Mama said. "But every time you get sick, I remind myself that in heaven we will have a new kind of body and nobody will ever be sick."

"Then I can't wait for heaven, either," Frank agreed. He leaned over the steaming pot and tried to inhale deeply. Isabel heard him wheeze. Exhausted, he moved to lie back on his pillow once again. "When I get to heaven, I want new lungs and a new chest and a new head."

"And you shall have them all," Mama answered. "I'll get rid of my knee that creaks every time I bend over. Daddy will have new eyes, so he won't need his glasses anymore. And the best part is, we'll be together."

"Will we live in a house or an apartment?"

"We'll have a mansion," Mama said brightly. "It will be the best place we ever lived."

"I want to go there," Frank said, "but not just yet."

No, not yet, Isabel thought.

Kaneko came to visit.

"Are you sorry we didn't go to the fight?" Kaneko asked.

"I am if you are," Frank answered. He smiled weakly. "Are you?"

"I am if you are," came Kaneko's response. He laughed. "Do you know that Harry and the others did not even get there before it was over? They were still trying to figure out how to get past the ticket gate, and all the people started coming out."

Frank managed a painful laugh. "I thought they had it all figured out before they left. Butch was bragging that he's done it so many times."

Kaneko shook his head. "It turns out he never has gotten past the ticket gate. In fact, the man collecting tickets recognized him and yelled at him before he even tried to sneak in."

"Then I'm glad we didn't go," Frank said.

"If you are, I am, too."

"Do you think I got sick because I was thinking about sneaking into the fight?"

Kaneko shook his head. "No, because then I would be sick, too."

"Good," Frank said. "But I'm not ever going to try that again. Are you?"

"I won't if you won't."

Frank turned his head to put his face against the cool pillow. "I think I have to go to sleep now, Kaneko. Will you come again?"

Alice and Daddy had gone to work in the morning. Mama wanted to stay with Frank as much as she could. Steven finally convinced her she should go to her own bed for some real sleep, while he stayed with Frank. That left Isabel to look after Audrey and the twins.

Audrey was not difficult to look after. She was eight years old and read like a twelve-year-old. She had never lost the stubborn streak she had had when she was little, but at least now she was stubborn about things like reading. Isabel gave her two novels that she had read in school last year, and Audrey was ready to settle in for the day.

The twins were a different story, however. Barb wanted to go to the park. Eddie wanted to play baseball. They would not take no for an answer. Isabel wanted the apartment to be quiet so Mama and Frank could sleep, so she took them out. At the park, Barb sat on a wooden swing and spun herself around so long that the chains wound themselves into a tight tangle. Isabel tossed a rubber ball at Eddie, who tried to hit it with a heavy stick and gleefully ran around imaginary bases whether he hit the ball or not. But all the while, she thought about Frank.

By lunchtime, Isabel was exhausted. The twins insisted they would only eat cookie sandwiches for lunch. Isabel would have let them, just to keep them quiet so Frank could rest, but there weren't any cookies in the kitchen. Instead, she cut chunks of cheddar cheese into perfect circles and laid them between two pieces of bread. Barbara was skeptical at first, but then she accepted Isabel's explanation that these were cheese cookie sandwiches. And whatever Barbara believed, Eddie accepted as well.

While they ate, Isabel went to check on Frank. Steven sat next to the window, reading. He shook his head in answer to her unspoken question. Frank was no better. Isabel rounded up Audrey from the girls' bedroom and made her pull her nose out of a book long enough to eat a cheese sandwich. At least the apartment was not like the inside of an oven the way it had been all week.

The afternoon hours stretched out so long that it seemed as if Daddy and Alice would never come home from work. But they finally did. Daddy took off his glasses for a minute and rubbed his tired eyes as he asked how Frank was doing.

"Has your mother called the doctor?" he asked.

Isabel shook her head.

"You're sure he's no better?"

"He sits up and talks a little bit, but he still can't breathe, and he still has a high fever," Isabel reported.

Daddy moved toward the phone on the kitchen wall. "I should call the doctor's office before they close for the day." He began to dial a number that was all too familiar.

At the last second, Isabel caught a glimpse of the twins tumbling through the living room toward Daddy. Quickly she moved to the doorway and blocked their entrance. She scooped up one twin under each arm and carried them, kicking and giggling, to the sofa. There, she continued to tickle them. She knew all their most ticklish spots. But she kept her ears open to hear what Daddy was saying from the other room.

"Yes, that's right, a high fever and difficulty breathing."

He paused.

"Yes, we've done all that. Nothing seems to help."

He listened to the voice on the other end.

"No, we certainly don't want that to happen."

Pause.

"Yes, of course, we'll do just as you say." Daddy hung up the phone.

Isabel stopped the tickling marathon. "What did they say?"

"We're to continue trying to cool off the fever, but if it's not better by morning, we'll have to take him in to see the doctor." Daddy rubbed the back of his neck as he sighed heavily. He moved toward the hall that led to Frank's room.

The doorbell rang just then. Barb and Eddie raced to be first to open the door.

"Hi, Kaneko," they squealed. "Where's Abiko?"

Kaneko's little brother was missing, but his mother was with him. Isabel tugged the twins away from the doorway.

"Hello, Mrs. Wakamutsu." She saw that her neighbor carried a tray covered with a pretty Japanese cloth.

"I bring a remedy," Mrs. Wakamutsu said quietly.

Kaneko quickly explained. "I told Mama how sick Frank is. She said that her brother used to get sick the same way back in Japan. She made the medicine that her mother used to make."

"Medicine?" Isabel asked.

"Special tea," Mrs. Wakamutsu said, dropping her eyes to the tray. "Special compress for Frank's chest."

Isabel stepped out of the doorway. "Please come in. I'll take you to see Frank."

In the bedroom, Daddy had his hand on Frank's head and was shaking his own head sadly. Frank's eyes fluttered open at the sound of more people entering the room.

"Someone to see you, Frank," Isabel said. "Kaneko is back, and he's brought his mother." She turned to Mama. "She has a Japanese remedy for Frank to try."

"It has always worked," Mrs. Wakamutsu said. "It never fails."

"A Japanese remedy?" Daddy asked, his eyebrows raised. "Is it medicine?"

"It is herbs," Mrs. Wakamutsu answered, "and roots. Nature's medicine."

Mama looked up at Daddy and then at Mrs. Wakamutsu. "Thank you. I know you would not want to hurt Frank. We would be glad to try your remedy."

Mama moved away from the bed, and Mrs. Wakamutsu took her place. She helped Frank to sit up a little better and then put the large teacup to his mouth.

"Drink it all," she instructed firmly.

Frank took a sip and grimaced. "It doesn't taste good."

"Taste is not important," Mrs. Wakamutsu insisted. "The tea will make you better, but you must drink it all."

Frank took another sip and swallowed. Gradually he drank the whole cup. Mrs. Wakamutsu returned the empty cup to her tray and picked up a compress of tea leaves and other ingredients.

"What's that goop?" Frank asked weakly.

"It's not goop," Kaneko said. "It's a compress. You have to put it on your chest, and it will help you breathe more easily."

Frank was doubtful and looked to his mother. Mama nodded. "Go ahead, Frank. We'll try it."

Silently, Mrs. Wakamutsu rubbed the warm, gooey mixture on Frank's thin chest. Then she helped him to lie back against his pillow again. Before getting up, she paused and bowed her head and closed her eyes.

"Is this part of the traditional remedy?" Isabel asked Kaneko quietly.

He shook his head. "No. She's praying for him. She always prays for someone who is sick."

Isabel sighed heavily. In all of her concern for Frank, she had not thought to simply pray for him. She closed her eyes and whispered a prayer for God to make Frank better soon.

At last, Mrs. Wakamutsu opened her eyes. "I will come again later. Frank should feel better in the morning."

It was another long night at the Harrington home. Alice prepared a simple supper of leftover chicken and a fresh salad. While the others ate in the kitchen, Isabel took plates of food to her parents. She knew they would not leave Frank long enough to eat, but she also knew it was important for them to eat. Frank was sleeping. Isabel thought his breathing sounded a little better, but it was hard to be sure.

When it was more than an hour past their bedtimes, Isabel finally got Audrey and the twins settled into their beds. Audrey pleaded to be allowed to read one more chapter, and Isabel finally agreed. Then she returned to the kitchen to help Alice clean up. When she finally tumbled into her own bed, she was so tired she fell asleep immediately.

The morning light woke her, and her heart quickened. She had wanted to wake during the night to check on Frank, but she could see that she had slept through the entire night. Audrey and Barbara were still sleeping soundly, but Alice's bed was empty. Isabel threw back the covers and leaped out of bed. She dashed out of her room and into the boys' room. Ed was the only one still asleep. Frank's bed was empty.

They've taken him to the doctor already, Isabel told herself. *It must have been a terrible night.* She whirled around and flew toward the kitchen.

She burst into the room, anxious to ask where Frank was. Her eyes fixed on the kitchen table. There sat Frank looking pale and tired.

"Good morning, Isabel," Frank said. "I'm having oatmeal for breakfast. Do you want some?"

CHAPTER 13

Hard Choices

Isabel looked longingly out the window. She did not really mind going to school. As long as she and Yoshiko were in the same class, as they had been for three years, the days passed pleasantly enough. In the afternoons, they did their homework together and analyzed the day at the same time. They knew which students in the class were likely to score the highest on the exams. They knew which teachers would reduce their grades if assignments were turned in late. School gave them plenty to talk about.

But this late September day was an especially nice one, and it was hard to be inside. Isabel could look out the window and see that a breeze was stirring the air gently. The summer had been so hot—much hotter than what Seattle residents were used to. Even the most creative people in the neighborhood ran out of ideas for fighting the heat. All the water in the Puget Sound was not enough to cool things off.

Isabel had hoped all summer that Daddy would drive them all to the ocean coast of Washington. Surely it would be cooler there. Just one toe in the cold Pacific Ocean would have cooled off her whole body, she was sure of it. But they never went. Thankfully the fall had brought cooler air and breezes and the kind of weather that made Isabel want to run to her heart's content without ever feeling tired.

The teacher wrote a formula on the blackboard, and Isabel dutifully copied it into her notebook. It was something about how the angles of a triangle added up. She would have to ask Yoshiko about it later. Geometry did not have much appeal to Isabel when she could be outside among the changing leaves. Seattle had plenty of evergreen trees, but there were still quite a few trees that changed colors, and Isabel relished the view. For a few weeks every fall while the leaves were changing and dropping, Isabel would remember that she had come from Minneapolis, where the changing season was the signal to get ready for a snowy, windy winter.

Isabel glanced over at Yoshiko and saw that her friend was paying more attention to the teacher than she was. As she copied another formula into her notebook, Isabel realized that she had no idea what the teacher was talking about.

Across the hall, in his classroom, Frank shifted in his seat. Only one more half hour and the day would be over. Audrey loved school and read every book she could get her hands on. But Frank had a long list of things he would rather be doing. Steven had promised to play baseball with Frank and Kaneko that afternoon. Frank was ready to be outside, running around.

As he turned a page in his history book, Frank coughed. For a moment, his chest felt tight. Then he coughed again.

Across the aisle, Kaneko turned his head to look at his friend. When Mrs. Holt turned her back to write on the board, Kaneko leaned over.

"Are you all right, Frank?" he asked in a whisper.

Frank nodded. "I think so." But he coughed again, this time harder.

Mrs. Holt turned to look at him. "Are you all right, Mr. Harrington?"

"May I be excused to get a drink of water?" Frank asked. He tried to clear his throat.

"Yes, but come directly back," Mrs. Holt instructed sternly.

A snicker came from behind Frank. Harry muttered, "Just trying to get out of class for a few minutes."

Frank started to reply but changed his mind. Harry would not understand. With a glance at Kaneko, Frank got out of his seat and made his way out into the hallway, where he found a drinking fountain. After a few long drinks and several deep breaths, he felt better. He had not been sick since those days in July when it was so hot. That was almost two months ago. Mrs. Wakamutsu's tea had seemed to help. Maybe he would need more.

Frank dragged himself back into the classroom and took his seat. Kaneko leaned over.

"We're supposed to write the answers to the questions on page fifty-two," he said.

Frank turned to the page and picked up his pencil.

"Are you sure you're over that cough?" Kaneko whispered. "It sounded bad."

"I think I'll be fine," Frank assured him.

"If you're getting sick again," Kaneko said seriously, "I'll ask my mother to make you some more tea. I know she would be glad to do it."

"Aw, come on, Frank," Harry hissed from behind. "You don't really believe that some silly tea made by a Jap is the same as real medicine."

"But it made him well!" Kaneko insisted.

"It was just coincidence," Ira said, taking up Harry's side of the discussion.

Frank squirmed. He hated it when Harry made fun of Kaneko, but it happened all the time. When he wanted to, Harry could be very funny, and Frank liked to be with him at those times. Harry was a terrific storyteller—especially about all the great fights—and he knew more knock-knock jokes than anyone else Frank knew. Kaneko was so serious all of the time.

"Do you want some tea?" Kaneko asked Frank.

"Do you want some tea?" Harry and Ira mimicked together.

"Gentlemen, please!" came Mrs. Holt's firm voice.

Frank turned away from the other boys and concentrated on the questions on page fifty-two. He felt the back of his neck grow hot.

The bell finally rang. Frank gathered up his books and bolted for the door. Usually he waited for his sisters and the Wakamutsus. They all walked home together. But on that day, Harry and Ira were waiting for Frank on the steps outside the school.

"Gentlemen, please!" Harry squawked, in a perfect imitation of Mrs. Holt. Frank could not help but start laughing.

Harry pursed his lips together. "Ladies and gentlemen," he said, "you will now turn to page fifty-two and write grammatically correct answers to all of the questions you find on that page."

Frank laughed aloud. "Nobody told me the answers had to be grammatically correct."

Isabel appeared on the steps. "Have you seen Audrey yet?" she asked.

Frank shook his head.

"I'd better go look for her," Isabel said. She gave Frank a funny look, but she turned and walked back into the building.

Yoshiko, Kaneko, and Abiko had found each other and assembled at the bottom of the concrete steps.

"Have you heard anything about the fights lately?" Harry asked as he slung himself over the iron railing and landed with a thud in the grass below.

Frank shook his head. "Not too much."

"That's because you spend your afternoons with that chicken Japanese kid," Ira said. "You ought to come along with us one day. We'll show you some action."

Frank laughed. "You didn't get into that fight, either," he said.

"Only because it was over so fast," Harry insisted. "We would have gotten in by the second round."

Harry slung his knapsack over his shoulder and started walking across the school yard. "Coming?" he asked Frank.

For a split second, Frank glanced at Kaneko. Then he jumped into action. "Sure," he said to Harry and Ira. He fell into step beside them. He did not look back again.

Isabel returned with Audrey. The Wakamutsus were still waiting on the steps. "Where did Frank go now?" she asked.

Kaneko shrugged. "He left."

"Left? Without you?"

Kaneko nodded.

"What happened?"

"Nothing. It's okay."

Isabel peered across the school yard and saw Frank striding along between Harry and Ira.

"I can't believe he's going home with those two!" she exclaimed. "They are two of the meanest people I have ever met."

"Don't worry about it," Yoshiko said. She took Abiko's hand. "Come on, we should be getting home, too. Mama-san will wonder where we are."

"Let's catch up with him," Isabel said. "I'll talk some sense into him."

Kaneko shook his head. "No. He can walk home with anybody he wants to."

"Did he even bother to tell you what he was doing?" Isabel was becoming more indignant by the moment.

"He just wanted to walk with Harry and Ira, that's all." Kaneko's words were calm, but Isabel could see the hurt shining through his dark eyes.

"He shouldn't treat you this way," Isabel insisted. "It's not right."

"It's part of being Japanese," Yoshiko said quietly. "You wouldn't understand. It happens all the time."

"It's just plain rude, that's all it is, and it's not the way we do things in the Harrington family." Isabel tugged on Audrey's hand. "Come on, Audrey. If we run, we can catch him."

"I don't want to run," Audrey said. And no matter how hard Isabel pulled on her hand, Audrey would not move her feet any faster. Frank was soon out of sight.

When Isabel and Audrey reached their apartment, they found Frank had changed to play clothes and was looking for a lost shoe.

"Why are you changing clothes?" Isabel asked.

"Steven promised to play ball with me and Kaneko." Frank bent over and looked under the sofa. "Here it is!" He pulled out his left Keds shoe and shoved his foot into it.

"Why would Kaneko want to play with you?" Isabel asked, slamming her books down on the table.

Frank stared at her with his blue eyes. "Why wouldn't he? We play every day."

"But today is different. Something happened."

"I don't know what you're talking about." Frank sprung to his feet. "Steven is waiting for us. I have to get Kaneko."

Shaking her head, Isabel followed Frank out into the hall and down the stairs. Her curiosity was getting the best of her. What would Kaneko do?

Frank knocked on the Wakamutsu door and wiggled impatiently in the hallway. Standing behind him a few steps, Isabel could see that Abiko answered the door. Frank asked for Kaneko, and in a moment, Kaneko appeared.

"Steven's waiting for us," Frank said. "Get your bat."

"I thought you were going to go out with Ira and Harry," Kaneko said.

"Naw. I'd rather play with you. Besides, Harry has chores to do. He just talks big. So are you coming?"

Isabel looked for any sign of hesitation in Kaneko's face. None came. He accepted what Frank said.

"I'll get my bat and ball," Kaneko said. He ducked back into the apartment. When he reappeared, Yoshiko was with him.

"Mama-san wants you home for supper," Yoshiko called after her brother. She turned to Isabel. "Hi. Are you ready to work on our geometry?"

Isabel seethed. "I'm ready to go after Frank and swing a baseball bat—but not at a ball."

"Calm down, Isabel."

"Why did Kaneko go with him?"

"Because he wanted to play baseball, I suppose."

"After what Frank did to him?"

"Frank is Kaneko's best friend. There is forgiveness in friendship."

"Another Japanese expression."

"No, something my Sunday school teacher said."

"Oh."

"I'll get my books, and we can go study in your apartment," Yoshiko offered.

"All right," Isabel agreed. She did not say anything more about Frank. But she had a few words she was saving for her brother.

CHAPTER 14

Making Things Right

Isabel thumped her left foot against the leg of the chair at the dining room table. She chewed on the end of her pencil and idly flipped the pages of her geometry book. There was a homework assignment, she was sure of that. She just could not remember what it was. Her foot thumped harder. At that moment, she did not care very much about what a hypotenuse was or what the angles of a triangle were supposed to add up to.

She sighed and threw the pencil down between the pages of the book. Looking across the dining room table, she could see that Yoshiko had written neat answers that filled most of a sheet of paper. Isabel squinted at Yoshiko's open book. Was that page sixty-three or page sixty-eight? Her foot thumped a little faster.

Yoshiko looked up. "Isabel, what's the matter with you? I haven't seen you write down a single answer yet."

"I guess I can't concentrate."

"It would help if you were on the right page," Yoshiko observed.

Isabel looked at her book. "I'm on page sixty-three. Problems one through ten, right?" she said hopefully.

"We did that last week. The assignment is on page sixty-eight." Yoshiko bent her head over her paper and pondered the next problem.

Isabel casually flipped to page sixty-eight as if she had known all along that it was the right page and read the first problem to herself. When she concentrated, geometry was not really so difficult to understand. Sometimes she even liked it. Someday, when she was flying a plane, it would be useful. She pressed her lips together as she began to write her answer. Her foot now thumped rapidly and loudly against her chair leg. The table shook with the rhythm of her foot.

"Isabel!" Yoshiko said sternly.

Isabel looked up.

"I can't concentrate," her friend said. "And you're making my writing all squiggly when you jiggle the table. Why are you making so much noise, anyway?"

"I hadn't noticed," Isabel responded. But she forced her foot to stay still and took her pencil out of her mouth.

Yoshiko turned back to her homework. Isabel tapped her book several times with the end of her pencil. She sighed heavily. Yoshiko looked up again.

"Why don't you just say whatever is on your mind and get it over with?" Yoshiko suggested with a hint of impatience in her voice.

"I don't know what you're talking about," insisted Isabel.

"Admit it. You're upset about Frank."

"No, I'm not."

"Yes, you are."

"I have a good reason to be upset with him. And so do you! Look at the way he treated your own brother."

"You're taking everything too seriously. They're just boys."

"I'm not finished with Frank yet," Isabel said firmly. She glanced at the clock. "Why isn't he home yet, anyway?"

"They haven't even been gone an hour," Yoshiko reminded her. "Concentrate on your geometry, Isabel. Remember, we have an English essay to work on, too."

"I forgot about that. How long is it supposed to be?"

"Five hundred words."

"And the topic?"

"Didn't you hear anything the teacher said today?" Yoshiko asked with aggravation.

"It was such a nice day out. I couldn't concentrate."

"If you don't finish your homework, you'll spend the whole afternoon inside and miss the beautiful day completely."

Isabel sighed and turned back to her book. She had barely finished the first problem when Yoshiko closed her geometry book and took out a clean sheet of paper to begin her essay. Isabel looked at the clock every two minutes. The minute hand did not seem to be moving.

"I think the clock is stopped," she said.

"No, it's not," Yoshiko answered.

But Isabel got up from the table and went to stand under the clock on the dining room wall. From there, she could hear it ticking.

"It must be going slow," she said.

"No, it's not," Yoshiko said without lifting her eyes.

Finally the apartment door flew open, and Frank and Steven

burst in. Isabel was instantly alert and rose awkwardly out of her chair.

"That was a great catch today, Frank," Steven said, grinning. "You might actually turn into a decent baseball player when you're older."

"Can we play again tomorrow?"

"Absolutely." Steven tossed a ball to Frank, said hello to Yoshiko, and disappeared down the hall.

"It's about time you came home," Isabel muttered. She glared at Frank.

Frank turned to look at her. "It's not suppertime yet. I'm not late for anything."

"I've been waiting to talk to you."

"How was I supposed to know that?"

Yoshiko scraped back her chair and stood up. Stuffing her papers into her geometry book, she said, "I think I'm ready to leave. I'm almost done, anyway. I'll see you in the morning. Don't forget about your essay." And she left quickly, shaking her head at Isabel as she passed her.

When the door closed behind Yoshiko, Isabel turned to Frank.

"I can't believe my own brother would treat his best friend the way you treated Kaneko today."

"What do you mean?"

"I saw the way you sauntered off with Harry and Ira, leaving Kaneko to walk home by himself."

"He wasn't by himself. The rest of you were there."

"You know what I'm talking about," Isabel insisted.

"I can have other friends besides Kaneko," Frank said in his own defense.

"You could have invited Kaneko to walk with you, too."

Frank screwed up his face. "He wouldn't want to do that. Harry and Ira make fun of Kaneko. Today they were making fun of the tea that his mother made me when I was sick. They do that all the time."

"Did you try to stop them?"

"Well. . .no. It's hard to tell Harry what to do."

Isabel shook her finger at Frank. "Kaneko is your friend, and you let those other boys say whatever they want to about him. They make fun of the Japanese, but you still play with them. Then you come home and expect Kaneko to act like it never happened."

Frank hung his head and stared at his shoes. The ball moved slowly from one hand to the other. Finally he let it drop to the floor.

"You're right," he said. "Kaneko tells me all the time that the Japanese way is to respect other people. I guess I need to learn to be more like the Japanese."

"I'm glad you see my point," Isabel said with a sigh. "I think you should apologize to Kaneko."

"I'm going to do it right now," Frank said. "And in the morning, I'm going to tell Harry and Ira what I really think."

"And what if they laugh at you?" Isabel challenged.

"I won't care. The only thing I like about them is that they like the fights just as much as I do. It doesn't matter what they think about Kaneko."

"That's the spirit!" Isabel cheered.

Frank turned around and opened the door. Isabel followed him down the hall a few steps, watching his determination to do the right thing. Now maybe she would be able to concentrate on her homework.

In the morning, Isabel raced into the kitchen, stuffing papers into a book.

"Come on, Frank," she urged, "we're going to be late. Audrey is already waiting outside."

"We have plenty of time," Frank said, with a glance at the clock.

"Don't forget about talking to Harry and Ira before school," Isabel said.

"I didn't say I was going to do it before school."

"You said you were going to do it in the morning. You're not going to back out, are you?"

"No! I'm going to do it. But technically I can do it any time before noon."

Isabel scowled. "Don't get technical with me."

"All right, all right, I'm coming."

In front of the apartment building, they met up with Yoshiko, Kaneko, and Abiko. Frank and Kaneko fell into step with each other and led the way toward the school.

"I want to keep up with them today," Isabel said to Yoshiko. "I want to see what happens when Frank finds Harry and Ira."

"Kaneko told me what Frank plans to do," Yoshiko said. "You must have given him quite a speech yesterday."

"I just reminded him about who his true friends are—who he should be loyal to. And then he figured out for himself that the Japanese are right."

"About what?"

"Respect. He realized he was not treating Kaneko with very much respect. I guess I taught him a thing or two."

"You teach him with your words," Yoshiko said quietly, "but you do not teach him with your example."

"That doesn't sound like a Japanese saying," Isabel quipped.

"It's not. But it is what I see."

Isabel turned to her friend with a wrinkled forehead. "I don't understand."

"You see that Frank has treated Kaneko with disrespect, but you do not see that you must treat Frank with respect, too."

"Of course I respect Frank. He's my brother."

"But you try to trick him and make him do things he doesn't want to do," Yoshiko said.

"I'm just having a little fun. He's so easy to fool."

"Yes, he is easy to fool," Yoshiko agreed, "so it is easy to play games with him. But he also has a very good heart. He likes to help people, and he's very generous."

"I never thought of it that way. I remember what he did last winter for the homeless men. He's talking about doing it again this winter."

"He is your little brother," Yoshiko said, "but you must treat him with respect. That is the Japanese way, and it is also God's way."

Isabel sighed and slowed her steps. As much as she hated to admit it, Yoshiko was right.

Ahead of her at the street corner, Frank and Kaneko met up with Harry and Ira. Isabel watched intently as Frank shifted his lunch pail from one hand to the other and began to talk. As she and Yoshiko approached the cluster of boys, Isabel could see the faces of Harry and Ira. At first they stared at Frank in disbelief, hardly giving a glance to Kaneko. Then their lips curled up in sneers. Laughing, they trotted ahead of Frank and Kaneko and never looked back.

Now Isabel could see Frank's blanched expression. He had done what he promised to do, but she could see that it had not been easy. Next to him stood Kaneko, his face shining with gratitude.

"Did I mention," Yoshiko said, "that I think your brother is also very brave? Kaneko and I know what it feels like to be hated just because we are Japanese. But no one has ever done anything like that for Kaneko before. It is a true gift."

Isabel nodded. She had never seen Kaneko's face look that way before.

Frank put his arm around Kaneko's shoulder, and the boys continued toward school. Yoshiko and Isabel followed with Audrey and Abiko. Yoshiko's words rang in Isabel's ears: *That is the Japanese way, and it is also God's way.*

CHAPTER 15

Neighborhood Gossip

Isabel lumbered down the flight of stairs and out the back door of the apartment building. She carried the family's large wicker laundry basket. It was not heavy, but it was large enough that she had to turn it sideways to get it through the doorways.

The small yard behind the building was crisscrossed with laundry lines. Socks, shirts, and sheets were mixed in with towels and trousers. Clothes flapped in the breeze like proud flags. Except in the very coldest weather, the laundry yard was a place where the women in the building gathered. They hung their laundry to dry, and at the same time they chatted about the neighborhood news.

Yoshiko was already in the yard with her mother. The Wakamutsu laundry had just come from the wash, and they were only now hanging it to dry. Isabel's mother had sent her upstairs for the basket so that they could take their laundry down. The clothes had been hanging out most of the day. In the overcast skies of Seattle, laundry took a long time to dry. But as soon as Isabel arrived home from school, Mama declared that it was time to get the clothes off the line. So Isabel had gone to fetch the basket.

As she emerged from the building and entered the yard, Isabel heard a thwack, then felt a sting across the back of her legs.

"Ow!" she cried. She snatched up the bottom of her gray cotton shirt to examine her injury.

The giggle that came from behind her made her spin around. Yoshiko grinned at her, a damp towel in her hands and her black eyes flashing. She was poised to snap at Isabel again at the first opportunity.

"So you want to play that game, do you?" Isabel said. She scanned the line that the Harrington clothes hung from, searching for a weapon of her own. She snatched at a towel. It was too dry for good snapping.

Mama laughed. "You're out of luck, Isabel. Our things are dry already."

Isabel clicked her tongue in disappointment, while her friend continued to grin. She narrowed her eyes at Yoshiko in mock anger. "You'd better watch out. I will get my revenge!"

"You'd better pay attention, Yoshiko," one of the other women said. "I've known Isabel for three years, and she nearly always manages to get her way."

Mama laughed. "She certainly tries hard."

"Thanks, Mrs. Assimer," Yoshiko responded, "but I have a few tricks up my sleeve, too."

Mrs. Cimelli smiled through her dark eyes. "Isabel, if I were you, I'd get my things off the line right away. I wouldn't trust your friend here."

Isabel pulled off a clothespin that held a pair of her little brother's pants to the line. As she looked at them, it hardly seemed that little Eddie could be big enough to need those pants.

"I'll stop teasing Isabel when she stops teasing Frank," Yoshiko said.

"Then you'll be teasing Isabel for a good long time," Mama said. She pulled a sheet off the line and tossed it over Isabel's head.

Mrs. Sorensen poked her head out between two sheets. "You two girls would never do anything to hurt each other."

Mrs. Wakamutsu smiled. "Yoshiko is a good girl. Isabel sometimes is good, sometimes not."

Everyone in the yard burst into laughter at the pronouncement from the quiet Japanese woman. Isabel gasped at her friend's mother. Mrs. Wakamutsu rarely spoke out in public.

Mrs. Assimer smoothed a towel. "Lydia, I see Donald coming home quite late these days. Boeing must be very busy."

"Boeing is always busy," Mama answered, reaching for one of Steven's shirts.

"I'm sure they are," Mrs. Assimer answered. "But it seems worse than usual lately."

Mama shrugged. "Perhaps it is."

"It is not a good sign when Boeing is so busy," Mrs. Sorensen declared.

Isabel raised her eyebrows and turned to hear what her neighbor had to say.

"I hear a lot of talk about war," Mrs. Sorensen said. "If Boeing is so busy, perhaps it is because they are building planes for the war."

"Boeing builds civilian planes, too," Mama was quick to point out. "The Clippers will be up and flying soon. Most of the overtime has to do with getting the Clippers built on time to fulfill the contract. I'm sure they will be a popular way for people to travel to Europe. It will mean good business for Boeing."

Mrs. Cimelli sighed. "Ah, it would be wonderful to visit Italy again. And to go in an air boat—one can only dream."

"I'm not so sure I would go to Italy," said Mrs. Sorensen, "not as long as Mussolini is in charge of the country. He has already invaded Ethiopia. There is no telling what he will do next."

Mrs. Cimelli shook her head. "I admit I don't understand Mussolini. But not all Italians are like that."

Mrs. Assimer shook her head. "No one should be traveling to Europe these days. First Mussolini in Italy, then Hitler in Germany." With hands that had years of experience, she swiftly folded a sheet and laid it in her basket.

Isabel noticed that Mama's hands were moving more slowly now, and she kept her eyes on the clothespins instead of looking at the other women.

Mrs. Assimer continued. "Adolf Hitler cannot be trusted any more than Mussolini. Ever since the Germans invaded Austria in March, I have had a bad feeling in my bones about that man."

Mrs. Sorensen nodded in agreement. "I'm not sure what to think about any of the Germans anymore."

Isabel glanced at her mother. "Hitler is just one person," Mama said. "He doesn't represent all the German people any more than Mussolini represents all Italians."

"He's their leader. If he doesn't represent them, I don't know who does."

"Austria is one small country," Mrs. Cimelli said. "They

already speak German there. Does it really mean so much that the Germans invaded Austria?"

"Why don't you ask the Austrians how they feel about it? Or the Ethiopians, for that matter," Mrs. Assimer challenged.

Mrs. Sorensen had filled one basket and now placed her folded clothes in a second one. "At least it won't go any further," she said. "The British and the French leaders have met with Hitler. They say everyone wants peace. No one wants a war. The other countries will leave Germany alone as long as Hitler doesn't do anything else. Hitler has given his word."

"And you believe him? 'Peace for our time,' they say," Mrs. Assimer said. "But I don't trust the Germans, not any of them."

Mrs. Cimelli gave Mrs. Assimer a sharp look and darted her eyes at Lydia Harrington.

"I'm not talking about individual German people," Mrs. Assimer clarified. "I'm talking about Germany as a country."

Isabel held her breath, wondering what Mama would say next.

Mama draped several sheets over one arm and turned to Isabel. "I think I'll just take these upstairs and put them back on the beds. Can you get the rest of our things?"

"Sure, Mama," Isabel said quietly.

"I'll help," Yoshiko offered. "We're almost done with our things."

"Thank you, Yoshiko," Mama said as she turned to go.

Isabel and Yoshiko looked at each other from the corners of their eyes as they worked side by side along the clothesline. Isabel pulled down her brothers' shirts, while Yoshiko carefully folded Audrey's school dresses and Barbara's play outfits.

Mrs. Wakamutsu hiked her basket to her hip. "I must go now, Yoshiko. Come home to eat."

121

"Yes, Mama-san," Yoshiko said, giving her mother a slight bow.

Yoshiko and Isabel worked at one end of the yard, while Mrs. Assimer, Mrs. Sorensen, and Mrs. Cimelli worked on the other side. A wall of billowing sheets separated them. The girls did not talk.

"Mrs. Wakamutsu is very nice," Mrs. Sorensen said, "but Japan is another country that I'm worried about."

"I know what you mean," Mrs. Assimer said. "I like the Wakamutsus as much as you do. They have been wonderful landlords. I couldn't ask for a better building to live in. They take care of everything meticulously. But Japan is trying to take over China. There may be a war in Asia, as well as in Europe."

"And if there is a war against Japan, how will we know which side all the Japanese people living in America will be on? Many of them come here to make money and send it back to Japan."

"I'd hate to think that Mr. Wakamutsu was doing that."

Isabel snapped her head around to look at Yoshiko. Her friend was quietly folding clothes. Isabel could hardly believe Yoshiko did not speak up. The neighbor women must have thought that Yoshiko had gone in the building with her mother. Isabel threw down Frank's best Sunday shirt and put her hands on her hips.

Yoshiko silently shook her head. "No, Isabel," she said so quietly that Isabel could barely hear her.

"How can you stand here and listen to that?" hissed Isabel.

"It is the best way," Yoshiko responded. "To say anything would only be bubbles on the water."

"Huh?"

"It's a—"

"I know. It's a Japanese expression. What does it mean?"

"It means that your effort would be in vain. Bubbles on the water are nothing, really, just air that is in that place temporarily."

"But I can't stand here and listen to them talk like that about the Japanese or about the Germans."

"They will not listen to you," Yoshiko whispered. "These are our neighbors, my parents' tenants. They do not mean to hurt your mother or me. Why should we stir up trouble that is not really there?"

"How can you be so sure about that?" Isabel calmed down enough to fold Frank's shirt properly.

A sheet flapped in the autumn wind.

"At least if there is a war, it will be on the other side of the world," Mrs. Assimer said. "It shouldn't matter to America, anyway."

"I suppose you're right," Mrs. Sorensen agreed. "If Europe wants to tear itself up, there is nothing we can do about it."

"The same goes for Asia," Mrs. Assimer responded.

"There is no reason for America to be involved," Mrs. Sorensen said. "It wouldn't be our war."

"None of our business," agreed Mrs. Assimer.

"But if there is a war in Europe," Mrs. Cimelli protested, "I will never be able to see my homeland again. I want to take my children there someday."

"Then you had better pray for peace," Mrs. Assimer said as she took down the last of her laundry. "As for me, I'm going to mind my own business and go in and feed my family their supper."

She pushed aside a billowing sheet and came face to face with Isabel and Yoshiko.

"I thought the two of you were long gone," Mrs. Assimer said. Her voice was friendly, and she smiled.

Isabel clamped her teeth together. "Our mothers left," she said firmly. "We stayed to finish the job." She ignored the touch of Yoshiko's hand on her arm. "Even German and Japanese families need clean clothes."

"I certainly hope you didn't take offense at anything we said. Of course we weren't talking about you."

"No?" Isabel challenged.

Yoshiko dug her nails into Isabel's forearm until Isabel could no longer ignore her.

Yoshiko smiled at Mrs. Assimer. "Have a nice evening, Mrs. Assimer."

"Thank you, Yoshiko, I will."

Isabel glared at Yoshiko as Mrs. Assimer walked away and disappeared into the building.

CHAPTER 16

Isabel's Joke

"Let's go! Let's go!" Barbara repeated the words she had been chanting for almost an hour.

Ed joined in. "Halloween party! Halloween party!"

Isabel winced at the noise. Eddie was dressed up like an alien from Mars. Even his face was green. Barbara had insisted on being a queen. She had been tapping Isabel on the shoulder with her cardboard scepter most of the afternoon.

Audrey, dressed as a hobo, rolled her eyes and said, "I'll meet you outside." She left the noisy Harrington apartment.

"Let's go! Let's go!" the twins screeched.

"Mama," groaned Isabel. "They're making me crazy."

"I know, I know," Mama said, coming into the living room. "I'm ready now." She smoothed her skirt, straightened her sweater, and glanced at the twins. "Eddie, you've got a smudge on your shirt already."

"Sorry," Ed mumbled.

"Never mind," Mama said. "You'll just have to be a dirty Martian. We don't have time to make another costume for you."

"Please, Mama," Isabel urged. "Just go."

"Are you sure you'll be all right alone here?"

"I'm fine, Mama."

"And you'll do the dusting?"

"Yes, I'll dust."

"I'm going to stop downstairs and tell Frank to come up in a few minutes so you won't be alone for long. And Steven will be home in a couple of hours. Daddy and I will just be across the street at the Jenkins's."

"I know, I know," Isabel said, taking her mother by the elbow and steering her toward the doorway. "Dust. Frank. Steven. Everything will be fine. Go and have a good time."

Mama laughed. "It will be fun! I'm only sorry I didn't have time to make myself a costume."

"Mama, you're too old!" Isabel said.

Mama shook her head. "No one is ever too old for a party. Remember that."

Finally they were gone. Isabel breathed a sigh of relief. She hoped Frank would not come upstairs from Kaneko's apartment very soon. It was not often that Isabel had the whole Harrington apartment to herself. Even if she did have to dust the furniture, she intended to enjoy the peace.

"How about a little dusting music?" she said aloud to herself. She went to the large console radio that sat prominently between two comfortable chairs in the living room and turned a knob. Dance music crackled through the air. With a dust rag in one hand, Isabel began to sway back and forth. She closed her eyes and twirled around, wondering what it would be like to go to a real dance and dance with a real boy.

The song ended. Isabel stopped swaying and brought the dust rag down on top of the end table. She moved it around half-heartedly, waiting for the next song to begin.

Instead, she heard: "Ladies and gentlemen, the director of the Mercury Theater and director of these broadcasts: Orson Welles."

Isabel sighed. A theater program! What about more music? But she made no move to turn off the radio.

A deep voice came on. "We know now that in the early years of the twentieth century, this world was being watched closely by intelligences greater than man's, yet as mortal as his own."

Isabel turned her head toward the radio. What was this man talking about? Her swirling movement in the dust slowed down. Orson Welles used some fancy words to talk more about Earth. But mostly he was talking about Mars. Isabel thought of little Eddie and his green Martian outfit. Isabel did not think there could really be living beings on Mars, but Orson Welles certainly made it seem possible.

As Isabel moved to another table with her dust rag, a weather report came on. Another voice reported an atmospheric disturbance of "undetermined origin" over Nova Scotia in Canada.

Now the announcer said that the program would continue with music from the Meridian Room of the Park Plaza in New York City.

"Good," Isabel said aloud. The music came on, and she moved around the room rhythmically with the beat of the music. Suddenly the music stopped right in the middle of a song. Isabel groaned.

"Ladies and gentlemen," a voice said, "we interrupt our program of dance music to bring you a special bulletin from the Intercontinental Radio News. At twenty minutes before eight, central time, a professor from the Mount Jennings Observatory, Chicago, Illinois, was observing several explosions of incandescent gas occurring on the planet Mars. The spectroscope indicates the gas to be hydrogen and moving toward the earth with enormous velocity."

Isabel stood still in the middle of the room. She sucked in her breath. An explosion on Mars? Gas moving toward the earth? Suddenly she began to giggle. She remembered that she was listening to the Mercury Theater program. It was all a Halloween trick! The people were probably not even really there.

The music came back on. A song finished, and people clapped—the people at the Meridian Room of the Park Plaza in New York City, Isabel supposed. No, she told herself, this is a theater program.

"A tune that never loses flavor," a voice said, "the ever popular 'Stardust.' "

This was a strange program, Isabel decided. Was it going to be dance music, or was it going to be a theater presentation? As the song played, Isabel moved around the living room with her dust rag. Then she moved into the dining room, where she could still hear the radio.

The music was interrupted again. This time a man announced that the government was asking the major observatories around the country to monitor the planet Mars. He promised an interview with a famous scientist in a few minutes. Then the music came back on.

Isabel's mouth began to twist in a smile. She glanced at the clock on the dining room wall. Frank ought to be coming home in a few minutes. Isabel had an idea! She stood in the dining room, grinning to herself.

When the door opened and Frank entered, Isabel knew what to do.

"Frank! There was an explosion on Mars! Dangerous gas is coming toward the earth. The Martians are invading!" She clutched his arm with both hands, digging her fingernails into his shirtsleeve.

Frank looked doubtful. "You're just talking about Eddie. I saw him leave a few minutes ago. Don't worry, you're safe. I thought he looked cute but not very scary."

"I'm not talking about Eddie," Isabel insisted. Music played in the background. "I heard it on the radio. They inter-rupted the music to announce it. They're going to interview a scientist and everything!"

Isabel had caught Frank's attention.

"You heard it on the radio?"

She nodded vigorously.

Frank stepped across the living room and inspected the radio dial. "You have it set to the CBS station."

"That's right."

"Daddy likes to listen to the news on CBS. He says it's the most reliable on the airwaves."

"He says that all the time," Isabel agreed.

"Are they going to have news again?" Frank asked.

"As soon as the scientist can come on," Isabel answered.

The music crackled and then stopped.

"There!" Isabel cried. "They're going to say more."

Frank sat in the chair nearest the radio and listened intently.

"We're now ready to take you to the Princeton Observatory," the voice said.

Making sure to keep a frightened look on her face, Isabel watched Frank. He bit his lower lip as he listened to the interview with the professor at the Princeton Observatory. Isabel could tell he was trying to make sense out of what he was hearing.

"Tell us what you see," the news commentator urged.

The professor described a red disk swimming in a blue sea. The planet was small and bright, with stripes across it.

"How far is Mars from the earth?" the commentator asked.

"Approximately forty million miles," the professor responded.

The interview was interrupted when someone handed the professor a message. The commentator urged him to read the message to everyone listening.

"Nine-fifteen, Eastern Standard Time. A seismograph registered a shock of almost earthquake intensity occurring within a radius of twenty miles of Princeton. Please investigate."

Frank's mouth dropped open, and he turned toward Isabel. "An earthquake?"

Isabel widened her eyes. "Do you think it has anything to do with the explosion on Mars?"

"I don't know," Frank said seriously. "I'm not a scientist."

Isabel could hardly hold in her laughter. Frank was doing just what she had hoped he would do.

"Listen!" Frank said. "They have a bulletin from Trenton, New Jersey."

The radio voice said, "It is reported that a huge flaming object believed to be a meteorite fell on a farm in the neighborhood of Grovers Mill, New Jersey, twenty-two miles from Trenton. A flash in the sky was visible within a radius of several hundred miles. The noise of the impact was heard as far north as Elizabeth."

The dance music came back on.

"How can they play dance music after news like that?" Frank wanted to know.

Isabel shrugged. "I'm sure they'll tell us more when they have more to say."

"Where's Elizabeth?" Frank asked.

"Elizabeth?"

"Elizabeth, New Jersey. How far is it from Trenton?"

"I don't know," Isabel said seriously. "It sounded like it was far away."

"That must have been an awfully big meteorite," Frank said. "That's probably what caused the earthquake."

"But what about the flash in the sky?" Isabel prodded. "What about the gas coming from Mars?" She put her hand over her mouth and gasped.

"What's the matter?" Frank asked, jumping to his feet.

"Maybe we should round up the rest of the family," Isabel said. "If there really is dangerous gas coming from Mars— what if they don't know? Mama and Daddy and the little kids are at a Halloween party. I don't even know where Steven and Alice are!" She sounded truly anxious.

"Calm down," Frank said. "Let's get some more information first."

"What about the Wakamutsus?" Isabel continued. "We have to let them know they might be in danger."

Frank scrunched up his face. "New Jersey is a long way from here. We're not in danger."

"But we could be," Isabel insisted.

Frank shook his head. "Probably the newspaper will have a big story about the meteorite in the morning. We can read about it then."

"But what about the flash on Mars? All the observatories are watching it. The Martians are coming!"

The color drained from Frank's cheeks. Isabel hid her face in her hands to keep from giving away the joke.

CHAPTER 17

The Tables Get Turned

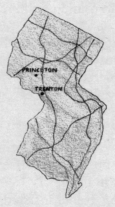

The music stopped. The reporter in New Jersey came back on the air and described what he was seeing: A huge cylinder, thirty yards in diameter, had crashed into the field in New Jersey. It was a yellowish color. No one had ever seen anything like it. The farmer who owned the field explained that he had heard a hissing sound. Then he saw a green streak before something smacked to the ground.

"That's no meteorite," Frank said.

"Then what is it?" Isabel asked. With a dramatic sigh, she dropped into the chair next to the radio, while Frank stood beside her.

"Maybe that scientist from Princeton will come back and

explain everything," Frank said hopefully.

"Keep back, keep back!" came the cries from the radio.

Frank could not keep himself from stepping back from the radio.

Inwardly Isabel laughed. Aloud, she gasped, "Was that an explosion? Did it explode? This is horrible!" She clapped her hand over her mouth in terror.

"It's the most terrifying thing I've ever witnessed," the reporter said. "Something's coming out, and another, and another. Ladies and gentlemen, it's indescribable! I can hardly force myself to keep looking at it."

"What is he talking about?" Isabel asked anxiously. "What's coming out? Is it the Martians? It's something really ugly, really horrible. It must be the Martians!"

The sound they heard next was undeniable. Isabel jumped in her seat—higher than she needed to.

"That was an explosion," Frank said. He moved in closer to the radio as the report continued. Everything was on fire. People were running and screaming everywhere.

The music came back on.

"Why did they do that?" Isabel pouted. "Who cares about the music now?"

Frank did not say anything. He simply turned around and walked out of the room.

"Where are you going?" Isabel called out. She was afraid that her joke had come to an end. "How can you leave now?"

Frank was rummaging through a cabinet in the hall. "I'm looking for a map," he said.

"Are you coming back?" Isabel glanced at the radio, hoping that the theater presentation would come back on soon. "Why do you need a map?"

"I want to look at New Jersey," came Frank's muffled response. Isabel could heard him moving papers and books around. Finally he came back to the living room.

"Got it," he said, holding an atlas over his head. "I want to find out about these towns they are talking about."

He opened the atlas and laid it on the living room floor. Together, Frank and Isabel crouched over it while he looked for the page showing New Jersey.

"There's Trenton," Frank said, putting his finger on the map. "It's right on the border with Pennsylvania. He moved his finger a little to the northeast. "And here's Princeton, not too far away."

"What about Elizabeth?" Isabel asked. "They said the noise was heard all the way in Elizabeth."

Frank studied the map and moved his finger again. "That's way up here, almost to New York City. That is a long way." He pressed his lips together, puzzled. "But I can't find Grovers Mill. It should be right around Trenton." He stretched out flat on the floor to get his face closer to the map. "It's just not here."

Isabel's stomach tightened. There was no cylinder, there were no Martians. There probably was no Grovers Mill, New Jersey, either.

"Maybe it's just too small to be on the map. It's just a little farm town."

"This is the best atlas Daddy could find," Frank said. "It's supposed to have everything on it."

"Oh, well, it doesn't really matter anyway," Isabel said.

Frank turned to her. "Why doesn't it matter? Don't you care about what's happening?" Isabel did not seem as worried as she had a few minutes ago.

"Well, yes. . .but. . ." Isabel was not sure what to say.

The music was interrupted by a news bulletin once again. The reporter said that at least forty people, including six state troopers, had been killed. The area was under martial law, and no one was permitted to enter. The state militia was spreading through the countryside to urge people to leave their homes and go somewhere safe. The strange creatures had crawled back into the cylinder and made no effort to stop the firemen.

Frank was starting to get suspicious. Looking over at Isabel, he waited to see how she would react to the news of the deaths in New Jersey. Isabel looked like she was thinking very hard. When they'd been lost on Mt. Rainier, Frank had seen what Isabel's face looked like when she was worried. And she did not look like that right now. Frank got up, went to the radio dial, and began to turn it.

"What are you doing?" Isabel asked.

"I just wondered what the other stations are saying about this," Frank said.

"But CBS is the best. You know that."

Frank did not answer. As he turned the dial, he heard the usual programs that his family often listened to in the evenings: music, game shows, city news. No one mentioned Grovers Mill, New Jersey.

"Why isn't anyone else talking about it?" Frank asked, continuing to turn the dial. "All the stations should be broadcasting something about what's happening."

"Just put it back on CBS," Isabel pleaded. "We have to listen to it. The world could be coming to an end. Wouldn't you want to know if that was happening?"

Now Isabel sounded worried again—maybe a little too worried. Frank studied his sister's face. The words she was saying sounded like she was frightened, but her eyes were shining. He had seen that expression before. Usually it meant that Isabel was scheming to play a trick on him.

Frank looked back at the radio as he turned the dial back to CBS. He was not sure what to believe. On the one hand, even Isabel, with all her crazy ideas, could not control what was on the radio. On the other hand, as she reminded him, it was CBS, Daddy's favorite news station. Daddy trusted CBS, so Frank had always trusted it, too.

When he found the CBS station again, the announcer was speaking in a somber tone. "Incredible as it may seem, both the observations of science and the evidence of our eyes lead to the inescapable assumption that those strange beings who landed in the Jersey farmlands tonight are the vanguard of an invading army from the planet Mars."

Seven thousand armed men had closed in on the cylinder in an attempt to destroy it. Only 120 had survived. The rest had been crushed under the metal feet of the monster and burned with heat rays.

Frank and Isabel continued to listen intently, but Frank was getting restless. Something was not right. He moved toward the window and looked out into the street. A trail of trick-or-treaters moved down the street, but nothing was unusual.

A few minutes later, the announcer said that coon hunters had found a second cylinder. The army was going to try to blow it up before it could be opened and more creatures released. Planes circled overhead where the creatures from the first cylinder were moving. They were great machines, enormous and powerful, moving across New Jersey toward the Passaic River.

"Their evident objective is New York City," the announcer said.

"New York City!" Isabel exclaimed. "If they get to New York City, I hate to think what could happen. They have to be stopped."

Frank decided what to do. He nodded seriously. "I think you're right. We have to go find Mama and Daddy. We have to warn the Wakamutsus."

"Do you really think so?" Isabel asked.

"Yes, and we must hurry. We should get some supplies together, too."

"Supplies?"

"Things that we need in an emergency," Frank said, watching his sister carefully. "Water, food, matches, stuff like that."

The radio broadcast continued, describing the millions of people trying to escape from New York City. The highways were jammed, the boats in the harbor overloaded. The army was wiped out. People were holding church services. Five great alien machines were now marching through New York City, destroying everything in sight. One walked through the Hudson River like an ordinary person wades through a brook.

Frank was ignoring the broadcast now and moving around the apartment. He found two empty milk jugs and filled them with water from the kitchen sink. Then he filled a canvas bag with canned food, making sure to pack a can opener, too.

Isabel followed him into the kitchen.

"Pack another bag of food," Frank said, "and grab some jackets for everyone in the family."

"Let's not be rash," she said. Isabel took the canvas sack from Frank and set it on the table.

"We might not ever come back here," Frank said. "We have to be prepared for anything."

"New York City is a long way from Seattle," Isabel said. "Those Martian machines will never get to us here."

Frank did not believe there were any Martian machines. But he was not going to give Isabel the pleasure of having fooled him again.

He picked up the canvas bag, slung it over one shoulder, and grabbed a water jug. "I'm going to find Mama and the others," he said. "Are you coming or not?"

Isabel hesitated. If Mama found out that she had played this trick on Frank and frightened him so badly, Isabel would not be allowed to leave the apartment until Christmas.

"I'm going," Frank said. Inside he was grinning, but he

kept his face straight.

"Don't go," Isabel pleaded.

"You can come with me if you want to," Frank said.

"I don't think we should go."

"Then you stay. But I'm going."

"Please, don't do that."

"Are you afraid to stay alone?" Frank asked.

"No, of course not."

"You should be. The Martians are coming. You heard it on the radio yourself."

Isabel hung her head. "Frank, the Martians are not coming."

"But it's on CBS, Isabel."

"I know. It's just a show. A Halloween prank."

He shook his head. "No, those scientists they interviewed are too smart to be fooled by a Halloween prank."

"There aren't any scientists, Frank. It's a theater program. Orson Welles and the Mercury Theater."

"Don't try to trick me, Isabel. This isn't funny." He moved toward the doorway.

Isabel lunged after him and grabbed his arm. "I'm telling the truth, Frank."

A smile escaped Frank's lips. "I know. I figured that out a long time ago."

"You did?" Isabel seemed genuinely surprised.

"I'm not a little kid anymore, Isabel," Frank said. "I've learned that when things don't make sense, you probably have something to do with it."

"But, Frank—"

"Admit it, Isabel. You were trying to scare me."

"Well, it was just a little Halloween fun."

Frank handed Isabel the canvas bag of food. "And I had a little fun, too. Now you can put all the stuff away."

CHAPTER 18

Moving Day

"Barbara, get out of there," Isabel ordered. "I'm trying to pack that box."

"I'm just trying to help," Barbara said.

"By getting into every box I open? You're going to ride in the car with the people, not in the truck with the boxes." Isabel reached for another empty box and set it on the kitchen floor in front of Barbara. "Here, you pack this one. Put your toys in it."

"I want one, too," Eddie insisted. Isabel found her brother a box.

Mama came back into the kitchen with an armload of towels. "We can wrap the dishes in these," she said. "That way they won't break."

"Are we moving today?" Barbara asked.

"No, not today," Mama explained. "It's almost bedtime. But in the morning Daddy's friend with the truck is going to come."

"And then we'll move to the new house?"

"That's right."

"Is Abiko moving with us?" Barbara wanted to know.

Mama shook her head. "No, but we're not moving very far. We'll be able to see the Wakamutsus as often as we like."

Frank came into the kitchen, balancing a tower of four boxes. He could hardly see where he was going. And he did not see Barb's rag doll on the floor. When he stepped on it, his foot slipped out in front of him. The boxes crashed to the floor on top of him.

Eddie giggled. "Boom! Like the bombs!"

Frank did not think it was very funny.

"It was only a year and a half ago that the union workers were striking," Mama said, "and Eddie was blowing up his blocks."

"I was glad when they got all their problems settled," Isabel said. "It's hard to believe more than a year has gone by."

Frank pulled himself to his feet. "And now we're moving."

Isabel chuckled. "I remember when we moved to Seattle from Minneapolis," she said. "We sold almost everything we owned."

"It was the only way we could afford to move," Mama said. "I'm not sorry. God has given us back everything we lost, and then extra blessings, too."

"Don't you miss your family?" Isabel asked.

"Sometimes," Mama answered, "but now we have the

Wakamutsus. If we hadn't moved out here, we wouldn't have met them."

"I'm glad you found a house close by," Frank said. "I already told Kaneko he can come and visit all the time. Maybe he can even sleep over."

"Are we going to have our own yard?" Barbara asked.

"Absolutely," Mama answered. "There's even a swing hanging from the tree in the back."

"Am I going to have my own room?" Barbara continued.

Mama chuckled. "I'm afraid there are still too many of us for that! But you'll have more room for your toys."

A knock came on the front door of the apartment and echoed through the empty rooms.

"I'll get it!" Eddie sprinted off toward the door before anyone could stop him. In a moment, he was back with all the Wakamutsus.

"We came to say good-bye," Yoshiko said, "and to wish you happiness in your new home."

Mrs. Wakamutsu stepped forward with a box of Japanese teas. "For good health," she said, "and to make happy memories."

Mama took the teas. "Thank you, Idori. Whenever I have a cup of tea, I'll think of you. And I hope you will come often to share a pot of tea with me."

Mrs. Wakamutsu nodded and smiled awkwardly. "I will come. I will come."

"This is for you, Frank," Kaneko said, handing Frank an envelope.

Frank tore it open. "It's a program from the big fight!" he exclaimed. "How did you get this?"

Kaneko smiled. "I have my ways. I've had it for a few weeks. I wanted to wait for the right moment to give it to you. Now you will remember me when you see the program."

Isabel looked at Yoshiko as a lump formed in her throat.

141

"I have something for you," Yoshiko said. She reached into her skirt pocket and pulled out something small. "Hold out your hand."

Isabel did as she was told. Yoshiko opened her fist and let the small, hard item fall into Isabel's palm.

"It's half a penny!" Isabel said. "How did you cut a penny in half?"

"We have some very good scissors!" Yoshiko answered.

"But why are you giving me half a penny?"

"I have the other half," Yoshiko explained. "When I look at it, I'll think of you. When you look at yours, you'll think of me."

"But we'll still see each other," Isabel protested.

Yoshiko nodded. "I know. But that will never be the same as having my best friend living just upstairs."

"It won't ever matter where we live," Isabel said. "You're my friend, and that's all there is to it."

Eddie was stacking empty boxes in a corner of the kitchen, getting ready to kick out the bottom one. Isabel winked at Yoshiko and walked over to Eddie's pile. As their mothers continued chatting, Isabel braced her foot up against the bottom box and put her hand on the top of the stack. Five-year-old Eddie, on the other side of his tower, swung his foot as hard as he could, but the pile did not fall. Puzzled, he kicked again.

Yoshiko rolled her eyes. Then she looked at Frank. "I guess she's got a new target now!"

There's More!

The American Adventure continues with *Rumblings of War.* The Harringtons have settled in their new home on Queen Anne Hill in Seattle, and both Frank and Audrey are facing problems.

Audrey tries to fit in with the other students at her new school by pretending that she doesn't know as much as she really does. Her grades drop, her parents are disappointed in her, and she feels miserable.

And as people become angrier about Japan's war against China, Frank doesn't know how to stand up for his Japanese-American friends. People are vandalizing Japanese-owned businesses and threatening Japanese Americans. Will Frank's friends be hurt? And what must Audrey do to be able to enjoy school once again?